Murder on the Ballarat Train

Also by Kerry Greenwood
Cocaine Blues
Flying Too High
Death at Victoria Dock
The Green Mill Murder
Blood and Circuses
Ruddy Gore
Urn Burial
Raisins and Almonds
Death Before Wicket
Away With the Fairies
Murder in Montparnasse
The Castlemaine Murders
Queen of the Flowers
Death by Water

Murder on the Ballarat Train

A Phryne Fisher Mystery

Kerry Greenwood

Poisoned Pen Press

Poisoned
Pen
Press

Poisoned Pen Press
6962 E. First Ave., Ste. 103
Scottsdale, AZ 85251
www.poisonedpenpress.com
info@poisonedpenpress.com

Printed in the United States of America

MYS
Greenwood K.

To Stephen D'Arcy
Car Jaume

Acknowledgements

To Jean Greenwood, for research, love and shoe-leather.
To Sue Rodger-Withers for jazz songs.

Chapter One

There was a beetle sitting next to the goat: (it was a very queer carriage full of passengers altogether)

Alice Through the Looking Glass,
Lewis Carroll

Fortunately, the Hon. Phryne Fisher was a light sleeper. She had dozed for most of the journey, but when the nauseating odour of chloroform impinged on her senses, she had sufficient presence of mind to realize that something was happening while she still had wits enough to react.

Reaching over the slumbering form of her maid and companion, Dot, she groped for and found her handbag. She dragged it open, moving as though she were five fathoms under water. The clasp of the handbag seemed impossibly complex, and finally, swearing under her breath and gasping for air, she tore it open with her teeth, extracted her Beretta .32 with which she always travelled, and waveringly took aim. She squeezed off a shot that broke the window.

It shattered into a thousand shards, spattering Phryne and Dot with glass, and admitting a great gush of cold air.

Phryne choked, coughed, and staggered to her feet. She hung out of the window until she was quite certain of her sobriety, then hauled the other window open. The train was still moving. Smoke blew back into her face. What was happening? Phryne reached into the picnic basket, found the bottle of cold tea, and took a refreshing swig. Dot was out to the world, slumped over her travelling bag, her long hair coming loose from its plait. Phryne listened carefully at her maid's mouth, with a cold fear in her heart. But Dot was breathing regularly and seemed only to be deeply asleep.

Phryne wet her handkerchief with the remains of the cold tea and opened the door of the compartment. A wave of chloroform struck her, and she had to duck back into her compartment, take a deep breath and hold it, before running into the corridor, tearing open a window and leaning through it. There was not a sound on the train; not a noise of human occupancy. She sucked in a breath and rushed to the next window, repeating the procedure until all the windows were as wide open as the railways allowed.

There were four compartments in this first-class carriage. She had noticed the occupants as she had sauntered along before supper; an elderly lady and her companion in the first, a harassed woman and three diabolical children in the second, and a young couple in the third. Phryne and Dot had occupied the fourth, and that probably explained their relative immunity, as the smell got thicker and harder to bear as Phryne neared the front of the train.

The engine halted; she heard the whistle, and an odd bumping noise at the front of the first-class carriage. There was a rush of steam, and the train began to move again, almost precipitating Phryne onto her knees, as she was still rather shaky. Still coughing and retching, she opened the window of the young couple, then the mother and the children. Finally she approached the first compartment, and the smell was strong enough to sting her eyes. She applied the wet handkerchief again, staining her face with tea, dived in and stood staring.

The companion lay flat on the floor with a spilt cup by her hand, but the window was already open and the old lady was gone.

Phryne then did something that she had always wanted to do. She pulled the communication cord as hard as she could.

The train screeched to a satisfying halt, and a porter came running, slapping open the door to the dining-car and immediately beginning to cough.

'Did you pull that cord, Miss?' he asked. 'For the love of Mike, what's been happening here?'

'Chloroform,' said Phryne. 'Help me get them out into the fresh air.'

The porter shouted, and several more liveried men crowded into the carriage, before they began to choke and tried to run out again.

'Idiots!' gasped Phryne. 'Put a wet hanky over your silly faces and come and help me.'

'I'll handle it, Miss,' said one rather tall and charming conductor. 'You'd better come out too, until it clears a little. Give me your hand, Miss, and down we go.' Phryne, who was feeling very unwell, allowed herself to be carried down the step and off the siding. She sat down unsteadily in cold wet grass and was delighted with the sensation. It seemed more real than the hot, thick darkness of the train.

The tall conductor laid Dot down beside Phryne, and the old woman's companion beside her. Dot turned over in deep sleep, her face against Phryne's neck, sniffed, croaked 'Nuit D'Amour', sneezed, and woke up.

'Lie still, Dot dear, we've had a strange experience. We are quite all right, and will be even better in a minute. Ah. Someone with sense.'

Phryne accepted a cup of hot, sugared tea from an intelligent steward and held it to Dot's lips.

'Here you are, old dear, take a few sips and you'll be as right as rain.'

'Oh, Miss, I feel that sick! Did I faint?' Dot supped some more tea, and recovered enough to sit up and take the cup.

'In a way, Dot, we all did. Someone, for some unknown reason, has chloroformed us. We were in the end carriage and thus we inhaled the slightest dose, though it was quite enough, as I'm sure you will agree. And when I get hold of the person who has done this,' continued Phryne, gulping her tea and getting to her feet, 'they will be sorry that they were ever born. All right now, Dot? I mean, all right to be left? I want to scout around a bit.'

'All right, Miss,' agreed Dot, and lay down in the dank grass, wishing that her head would stop swimming.

The train had come to a halt in utter darkness somewhere on the way to Ballarat. All around the pastures were flat, cold, and wet; it was the middle of winter. She regained the train as the guards were carrying out the last of the children, a limp and pitiful bundle.

'Well, this wasn't on the timetable!' she exclaimed to the nearest conductor. 'What happened? And who caused it to happen?'

'I thought that you might have seen something, Miss, since you were the only one awake. Though you seem to have caught a fair lungful of the stuff,' he added. 'You sure that you feel quite the thing, Miss?'

Phryne caught at the proffered arm thankfully.

'I'm quite all right, just a little wobbly in the under-pinnings. What are we going to do?'

'Well, Miss, the train-conductor thinks that we'd better put everyone on board as soon as they have recovered a bit and take the train on to the next town. There's a policeman there and they can send for a doctor. Some of them kids are in a bad way.'

'Yes, I expect that will be the best plan. I'll go and see if I can help. Give me an arm, will you? Do you know any artificial respiration?'

'Yes, Miss,' said the middle-aged man, glancing admiringly at the white face under the cloche hat. 'I learned it for lifesaving.'

'Come on, then, we've got lives to save. The children and the pregnant woman are the main risks.'

Phryne found, on examination, that the youngest child, a particularly devilish three year old on whom she had been wishing death all day was the worst affected. His face was flushed, and there seemed to be no breath in the little body. She caught the child up in her arms and squeezed him gently.

'Breathe, little monster,' she admonished him, 'and you shall dance on all my hats, and push Dot's shoes out the window. Breathe, pest, or I shall never forgive myself. Come on, child, breathe!'

In, out, the chest rose and fell. The child gulped air, choked, fell silent again, as Phryne jogged his chest and he dragged in another breath, with nerve-racking intervals in which she heard the other passengers groaning awake. The pregnant woman was retching violently, and abjuring her comatose husband to awake. A small hand clutched Phryne painfully by the nose and the child's strong legs flexed and kicked. The whole child seemed to gather himself for some final effort. Phryne held her breath. Was this a death tremor? Johnnie took his first independent breath.

'Waaaah!' he screamed, and Phryne began to laugh.

'Here, you take him,' she said to the nearest guard. 'But be careful, he'll be sick in a moment.'

The guard was a family man, and took the resultant mess philosophically. They were all awake now; the woman and the children, the pregnant lady and her husband, and Dot. All except the companion to the elderly lady, and she was burned about the nose and mouth and very deeply drugged, though her heart pounded strongly under Phryne's hand.

'All back on the train,' ordered the conductor. 'This way, ladies and gentlemen, and we'll soon have you comfortable. This is some sort of silly joke, and the Railways will be responsible for any damages. Might I offer you a hand, Miss er…'

'Fisher. The Hon. Phryne Fisher,' said Phryne, allowing herself to lean on the arm. 'I really am not feeling at all well. How long to Ballan?'

'About ten minutes, Miss, if you'll excuse the guard's van, there being no room in the rest of the train.'

Phryne and Dot sat side by side on the floor, next to a chained dog and a cage full of sleepy chickens. The lady-companion was laid beside them, and the rest of the first-class passengers sat around the walls, surveying each other with discomfort.

'I say, old girl, you look as if you'd been pulled through the hedge backwards,' opined the young husband in a feeble attempt at humour, and his pregnant lady rocketed into hysteria.

It took Phryne the ten minutes to Ballan to induce in the lady a reasonable frame of mind, and at the end of it Phryne was a rag.

'If you have anything else to say that you think is funny, I'll thank you to keep it to yourself,' she snarled at the husband, catching him a nasty accidental-on-purpose crack on the shins. 'I've got other things to do than calm the heeby-jeebies. Now we are at Ballan, Dot, I hope that we can get to the overnight things, for we really must have a hot bath and a change of clothes, or we shall catch our death.'

'There's a hotel in Ballan,' said the mother, catching little Johnnie as, much recovered, he poked his fingers in among the chickens, 'Come away, Johnnie, do!'

'The Railways can pay for it, then,' suggested the young man, with a wary eye on Phryne. 'I haven't got the cash for an overnight stay.'

'I can advance you enough,' said Phryne. 'Not to worry. Here comes our nice conductor to release us from durance fairly vile.'

The conductor had clearly done wonders in a very short time.

'If the ladies and gentlemen would care to break their journey for awhile, they may like to bathe and change at the hotel,' he suggested. 'The guards will bring your baggage. The hotel is about a hundred yards down the street, and we will carry the sick lady.'

Phryne took one child, Dot another, and they trailed wearily down the road to the Ballan Hotel, a guesthouse of some pretension. They were met at the door by a plump and distressed landlady who exclaimed over their condition and took charge of the children.

'Room two, ladies, there's a bath all ready for you. I'll send the man with the baggage when he arrives. I shall have tea ready directly, and I've sent for the doctor, he should be here soon.'

Dot and Phryne gained their room and Phryne began to strip off her wet garments. Dot located the bath, and gestured to it.

'You first—you were worse affected,' insisted Phryne, and Dot recognized inflexibility when she saw it. She took off her clothes in the bathroom and sank into the tub, feeling the aching cold ease out of her bones. She heard the door open and close as she lay back and shut her eyes, and presently there was Phryne's voice.

'Come on, old dear, you don't want to fall asleep again! I've got the clothes and I've got some tea.'

'In a minute,' promised Dot, and exchanged places with her mistress.

They were dressed in clean clothes and thoroughly warmed when the conductor returned to advise them that the chloroform vapour was all gone and they could resume their journey, if they liked. Phryne was ready to go, and was called in to rouse the companion of the elderly lady.

The woman was much scorched or scalded about the nose and mouth, and the doctor seemed worried about her. She had not begun to rouse until the injection of camphor had been made. Then she opened her eyes all of a sudden, and hearing Phryne's voice, asked, 'Where's Mother?'

And Mother was gone.

After that, there was no further chance of getting to Ballarat, and Phryne turned to the landlady.

'There was another lady on the train, and she has definitely gone. We must call the police—perhaps she fell out the window. Is there a police station in Ballan?'

'Yes, Miss, I'll send the boy around now. What a terrible thing! We'll have to rouse out some of the men to go searching.'

'Dot, are you better?' asked Phryne of her maid.

Dot replied, 'I'm still a bit woozy, Miss. What do you want me to do?'

'Go and make some tea.'

'I can manage that,' agreed Dot, and went out. The doctor was applying a soothing cream to the stricken woman's face.

'What burned her? Chloroform?' asked Phryne, as she took the jar out of the doctor's insecure hold and held it out for him to dip into. 'Does it burn like that?'

'Certainly. She has had a chloroform soaked cloth laid over her face, and if you hadn't woken them all up and got her out of the train, she would now be dead, and even so there may be permanent damage to her liver.'

'What about the rest of us? Would we have all been affected just by the chloroform in the first compartment?'

'No. The gas is heavy, much heavier than air, and very volatile. Someone must have poured it into the ventilation system. Someone wanted you all asleep, Miss Fisher, but I have no idea why. There now, you may stopper the jar. Poor woman, a nasty awakening, but she's slumped back into sleep again. Can you watch her for an hour? I should go and see how those children are getting along.'

'By all means,' agreed Phryne, her conscience still tender in the matter of little Johnnie. 'I'll stay here. If she wakes, can I give her tea?'

'If she wakes, Miss Fisher, you can give her anything you like,' said the doctor, and hefted his black bag in the direction of the children's room.

An hour later, at three in the morning, the woman awoke. Phryne saw her stir and mutter, and lifted her to moisten her lips with water.

'What happened? Where's Mother?' came the cracked voice, prevented only by bodily weakness from shrieking.

'Hush, hush now, you're safe, and they are out looking for your mother.'

'Who are you?' asked the woman dazedly. She saw Phryne's expensive dressing-gown, edged in fox fur, her Russian leather boots of rusty hue, and an aloof, pale, delicate face, framed in neat, short black hair and with penetrating green eyes. Next to this vision of modish loveliness was a plain young woman with plaits, dressed in a chenille gown like a bedspread.

'I'm Phryne Fisher and this is Dot Williams, my companion. Who are you?'

'Eunice Henderson,' murmured the woman. 'Pleased to meet you. Where is Mother? What is happening? And what's wrong with me? I can't have fainted. I never faint.'

'No, you didn't faint. We are in the Ballan hotel. Someone chloroformed us—the whole first-class carriage. I knew that I should have motored to Ballarat, but I do like trains, though I'm rapidly going off them at the moment. Luckily, I was in the last compartment, and I am a very light sleeper. I broke the window, and then opened all the others and dragged everyone out. You I found lying on the floor of the compartment, with a spilt glass near your hand, and there was no one else there, I can assure you. The window was open—could she have fallen out?'

'I suppose so—she is a thin little thing, Mother. I can't remember much. I was asleep, then I heard this thump, and I felt ever so ill, so I got up to get some water, and…that's all I can recall.'

'Well, never mind for the moment. There's nothing we can do until the searchers come back. They have roused the railwaymen and they've all gone walking back along the track. They'll find her if she is there. Why not go back to sleep? I'll wake you if anything happens.'

Eunice Henderson closed her eyes.

'Miss, she must have been the Eunice that the old lady was nagging all the time on the train,' whispered Dot, and Phryne nodded. The journey had been made unpleasant not only by the children, but also by an old woman's partially deaf whine in the forward compartment, as unceasing as a stream and as irritating as the mosquito which had caused Phryne's sleep to be so light. She had reflected during the journey that the mosquito was the lesser hazard, because it could be silenced with a vigorous puff of Flit.

'Eunice, the window is shut—you know that I hate stale air!' 'Eunice, the window is open—you know that I hate a draught!' 'Eunice, I want my tea!' 'Eunice, you are so slow!' 'Eunice, when do we get to Ballarat?' 'Eunice, are you listening?' 'Eunice, where's my novel? No, not that novel, you stupid girl, the one I was reading yesterday. What do you mean, you didn't bring it? What other mother has to endure such a stupid, graceless, uncaring daughter? At least you'll never marry, Eunice, you'll be with me until I die—and don't think you'll get all my money—don't frown at me, girl! No one loves a poor, deserted old woman! Eunice! Where are you going?'

Phryne thought that if Eunice had finally tipped Mother out the train, she could understand it. But it did not look as though she had. Surely Eunice would not have drugged the whole train—or burned herself so badly.

Under the burns and the soothing cream, Eunice was rather good looking. She had strong, clean features, rather masculine but well-formed, and curly brown hair kept firmly controlled under bandeau and net. Her eyes, Phryne remembered, were a rich brown, and she was long limbed and athletic. Why should her mother have been so sure that Eunice would never marry? Admittedly, there was a shortage of young men, and a superfluity of women, the War to End All Wars having slaughtered the manhood of the Empire, but they were there if one tried. Perhaps Eunice had never had the chance to try. Mother was a full-time career.

Dot poured herself another cup of tea and began to twist her plait into a knot, which meant that she was thinking.

'Miss, could she have…?'

'I don't think so, Dot, because of the burns. She didn't need to go through all this pretence. All she had to do was boost Mother out of the window, wait a few minutes, then stagger out into the corridor and faint. The train would be miles away by the time she 'recovered' and then all she had to do was gasp that Mother was looking out of the window, lost her grip and fell, and that would be that. No old lady would survive a fall from a fast moving train, at least, its unlikely. No. Someone altogether other has contrived this, and a clumsy attempt it is. The previous theory at least has the virtue of simplicity. This one is too elaborate and should not prove too hard to solve, if it is murder.'

'If it's murder, Miss? What else could it be?'

'Kidnapping? Some frolic that went wrong? I don't know, Dot. Let's wait until we see what develops. Would you like to take a short nap? I can watch for a while—I'm not sleepy.'

'Neither am I,' said Dot. 'I don't want to ever sleep again!'

◇◇◇

They watched until four in the morning, when a respectful, soft-footed maid came to ask if the Hon. Phryne Fisher could spare Sergeant Wallace a word.

Miss Fisher could. She rose from her seat on the floor and wrapped her cream dressing-gown around her and followed the maid into what looked to be the hotel's breakfast-room. Phryne was too tired to be hungry, but thought longingly of coffee.

Miraculously, the policeman had before him a full percolator and several cups. He poured one for Phryne and she sat sipping gratefully and breathing in the steam.

This sergeant was one of the large economy-sized policemen, being about six-and-a-half-feet tall and several axehandles across the shoulders. The Australian sun had scorched his milky Celtic complexion into the hue of council house brick. His light grey eyes, however, were bright and shrewd.

'Well, Miss Fisher, I'm Sergeant Wallace and I'm pleased to meet you. Detective-inspector Robinson says to give you his best regards.'

Phryne looked at this country cop over the edge of her coffee cup. He grinned.

'I telephoned the list of passengers to the central office an hour ago, Miss Fisher, and Robbo was on duty. He recognized the name. Thinks a great deal of you, he does. We went to school together,' he added. 'Geelong Grammar. I won a scholarship, however. How are you, Miss? Feeling more the thing?'

'Yes. But Miss Henderson is still very unwell—and worried about her mother. Have you found her?'

'Yes, Miss, we've found her all right.'

'Dead?'

'As a doornail. We brought her into Ballan a few minutes ago. Did you see her, Miss? To identify, I mean?'

'Yes, I saw her,' agreed Phryne. 'I would know her again.' She thought of the tiny, wizened figure, her thinning white hair carefully combed and dressed in a bun, her fingers laden with many emeralds.

'Would you do it, then, Miss? I'm only asking to spare Miss Henderson, and they have no near relations. And Robbo, I mean Detective-inspector Robinson, has a high opinion of your courage, Miss Fisher.'

'Very well. Let's get it over, then. Lead the way.'

The huge policeman shouldered his way out of the breakfast room into a cold yard, and thence into a stable smelling of dust and hay and horses.

'We put her in here for the moment, Miss,' he said solemnly. 'We'll take her into the Coroner's later. But I want to make sure that it's the right woman.'

He lifted the lamp high, casting a pool of soft golden light.

'Is this her, Miss Fisher?' he asked, and drew back the blanket from an untouched face.

'Yes,' said Phryne. 'Poor woman! How did she die?' As she spoke her hands touched the skull, and felt the terrible dent where consciousness had been crushed. The skin was clammy and chill in the way that only the dead are cold. The eyes were shut, and someone had bound up the jaw. Mrs. Henderson wore no expression now but peace and faint surprise. There was nothing here to shock Miss Henderson. Phryne said so.

'Maybe not from the face,' said the sergeant grimly. 'But have a look at the rest.'

Phryne drew off the blanket and stepped back a pace, astonished and sick. Such a fury had fallen on the old woman that scarcely a bone was whole. She was covered in red clay. Her limbs were broken, even her fingers twisted out of true, though no part of her seemed to be missing. She laid the blanket back over the wreck of a human creature and shook her head.

'What could have done that? Did a train run over her?'

'No, Miss. The doctor has a theory, but it's not a nice one.'

'Tell me, while we go back to the hotel,' she said, taking the sergeant's arm. He closed the stable door carefully and waited until Phryne was seated with a fresh cup of coffee before he said, 'The doctor reckons she was stamped on.'

'Stamped on?'

'Yes, Miss, by feet.'

'Ugh, Sergeant, I hope your doctor is wrong. What a dreadful thought! Who could have hated her that much?'

'Ah, there you have me, Miss. I don't know. Now tell me exactly what happened this night, from the time you got on the train.'

Phryne gathered her thoughts, and began.

'I boarded the train at six o'clock at Flinders Street Station with my companion Miss Williams, a bunch of narcissus, a picnic basket, a trunk, a suitcase, a hatbox and three novels for railway reading, intending to go to Ballarat to visit some of my cousins—the Reverend Mr. Fisher and his sisters. I believe that they are well known in the city and they were expecting me, so you can check with them, and tell them that I shall be along as soon as I can. We were seated in the fourth compartment of the first-class carriage. We saw to the baggage, then had a cup of tea and a biscuit from the dining car. There I made the acquaintance of Miss and Mrs. Henderson, and the woman with the children.'

'Mrs. Agnes Lilley, that is, Miss, and Johnnie, Ernest, and George.'

'Quite. Those children were the most pestilential set of little nuisances who ever afflicted a train. Mrs. Henderson found them particularly annoying, I thought. I had a few words with that poor old lady on the subject of modern children and how they should have all been drowned at birth, and then Dot and I went back to the compartment. We had some tea in the thermos and we didn't need to stay in the dining car. I noticed that the couple—'

'Mr. Alexander Cotton and his wife, Daisy,' put in the sergeant helpfully.

'Yes, she seemed ill and nervous, and he was bringing her a cup of tea. A clumsy young man. He spilled it all over a passing child and I refilled it from my flask so that he didn't need to go back to the dining car and doubtless spill it all over again. That sort of young man can continue being clumsy all night, if pressed. I also noticed that his wife is very pregnant, because I find expectant women uncomfortable travelling companions. I hoped that she wasn't going to deliver in the train, which I believe is not uncommon. Can I have some more coffee?'

'There's none left.' The sergeant pressed a bell, and the landlady came to the door.

'Could we have some more coffee, Mrs. Johnson? Is Doctor Heron still here?'

'Yes, Bill, the doctor's watching over one of them kids. He's worried about the youngest. I'll get some more coffee in a tick—shall I fetch the doctor?'

'No need at the moment, just catch him if he looks like going home. Thanks, Mrs. J.'

'I was reading one of my novels and Dot was asleep, and I dozed off over the pages with my light on, then I smelt chloroform. I woke up, and broke the window.'

'Why did you wake up, Miss Fisher? Everyone else just seems to have got sleepier.'

'I hate the smell of chloroform,' said Phryne, lighting a gasper to banish the remembrance. 'That sweet, cloying stench—ugh! I must have inhaled quite a lot, though, I could hardly move.'

'How did you break the window, Miss?'

'I hit it with my shoe,' lied Phryne, who was not going to disclose the presence of her pistol unless she had to. 'And I damaged the heel, blast it. A new shoe, too.'

Should the sergeant search, he would find Phryne's high-heeled shoe with window glass in the leather and glass damage to the heel. Phryne had carefully ruined the shoe on the way to Ballan. She believed in being just as truthful as was congruent with sense and convenience.

'Yes, and then what happened?' asked the sergeant.

'I staggered out and opened all the windows, and I pulled the communication cord.'

'Yes, Miss, that was at 7:20 p.m. The guard looked at his watch—Railways policy, evidently—and how long do you think that opening the windows took?'

'Oh, about ten minutes. I felt the train stop for a while when I was letting in the air.'

'Ah, yes, Miss, that times it. Water stop for three minutes at 7:15 p.m.'

'There was some sort of bump—I thought it came from the front of the train—but I was getting very wobbly by then.'

'I'm sure you acted very properly, Miss Fisher. If you hadn't broken that window, the whole carriage would have been gassed, and the doctor says that some of them kids would have been dead before the train got to Ballarat. A terrible thing, and Mrs. Henderson dead, too.'

'Can she have fallen out of the window, do you think?'

'Fallen or been dragged,' said the sergeant grimly. 'Here's the coffee. Thank you, Mrs. J.'

Mrs. Johnson withdrew reluctantly—it was not often that anything interesting happened in Ballan—and the sergeant poured more coffee for Phryne.

'What did you see, Miss, when you opened each compartment door?'

He got out his notebook and licked his pencil.

'In the compartment nearest me were Mr. and Mrs. Cotton. They seemed to have fallen under the influence together, for he had his arms around her and she had her face buried in his shoulder. They were half-conscious. Then there was Mrs. Lilley and her frightful children—she was stirring and moaning, but the

children were all dead to the world…what an unfortunate meta-
phor, I beg your pardon. In the first compartment the window
was open, Mrs. Henderson was gone, and Miss Henderson was
lying on the floor, prone, with a cloth half-over her face.'

'What was she wearing?'

'A skirt and blouse, and a woolly shawl. She had a spilled cup
near her hand, as though she had dropped it where she fell. The
smell of chloroform in that confined place was awful, it stung
my eyes until I could hardly see.'

'And then what did you do, Miss?'

'I pulled the communication cord and the guards came, and
we got everyone out of the train. Where is the train, by the way?
You can't have left it sitting on the line all this time, not if you
haven't closed the rail link altogether.'

'No, Miss, we haven't closed the line, not now we've found
the body. The rest of the train has gone on to Ballarat, but the
first-class carriage is still here in the siding, in case we can find
a clue. You didn't happen to notice anyone you didn't know
walking through the train, did you, Miss? After you came back
from the dining car.'

'Only a rather good looking young guard, blond, he was,
with a very nice smile.'

'A young man, Miss? I saw all the guards on that train, and
there was none of 'em under forty.'

'Are you sure?' demanded Phryne, who had a clear recollec-
tion of a rather ravishing young face under the cap; unlined,
smooth, tanned, and certainly not more than twenty-two or
-three years old.

'Quite sure,' responded the sergeant. 'Would you know this
man again, Miss?'

'I think so,' temporized Phryne. 'Perhaps. But you'd better
start looking for a blond young man, Sergeant, because I think
that he might be your murderer.'

Chapter Two

Then a very gentle voice in the distance said,
'She must be labelled "Lass, With Care",
you know—'
Alice Through the Looking Glass
Lewis Carroll

There was nothing to be done for the rest of the night but to recruit as much strength as possible. Phryne curled up in an armchair, and Dot went to lie on her bed. Miss Henderson awoke at intervals, was reassured, and lapsed back into sleep. Gradually the cold, before-dawn grey light seeped into the room, and Phryne dozed off.

Her dreams were most uncomfortable, and she was glad to wake. All through and around a peculiar series of events constructed by her bewildered subconscious was the picture of the old woman as she had last seen her; the broken limbs, the pathetically twisted fingers, bare and broken…Phryne said, 'Rings!' and woke herself up.

'Thank God for waking, I could not have stood that dream much longer. Her rings! All those emeralds, and they are gone. I must tell that nice sergeant, but first I must have a bath and some breakfast and find some clothes. I wonder how long we shall have to stay here? And how is Miss Henderson?'

Phryne bent over the patient, and found her sleeping normally, her face still and peaceful under the burns. Her heartbeat was strong and regular. Fairly soon she would have to know that her mother was dead, but with any luck Phryne would not be the one to tell her.

Phryne tiptoed into the room allotted to herself and Dot and found that her maid was awake and had run a bath, set out Phryne's clothes, and was herself washed and dressed.

Phryne shed her cream velvet and fox fur dressing-gown gratefully, pulled off her silk pyjamas, and subsided into the steam, scented with Phryne's favourite bath oil, 'Rêve du Coquette'.

She dried herself thoroughly, as though she could scour the memory of death off her skin with the hard hotel towelling, and dressed for what looked to be a cold, nasty winter's day in trousers of black fine-loomed wool, a silk shirt in emerald green, a jumper knitted with rather amusing cats, and the black cloche. She pulled on her red Russian boots and took a red outer coat of voluminous cut with deep pockets.

Dot was dressed in a long warm skirt and a woolly jacket in fine undyed fleece. She had a wheat coloured shirt and thick lisle stockings, but was still pinched and shivering.

'You should wear trousers, Dot, they are the only sensible clothing for this sort of weather.'

'Oh, no, Miss,' was all that Dot would reply through chattering teeth, so Phryne gave up and led the way into the breakfast-room. It was eight-thirty in the morning, and someone should surely be stirring.

The breakfast-room (which Phryne was sure would double as the dining-room) was a large room with bay windows, now looking out onto miserable cows and battered scrub. Every leaf was hung with dew, as the early fog condensed, and it was grey and chill, a suitable morning for the aftermath of a murder. However, the chafing dishes were set out next to a tall coffee-pot and all the makings for tea, and a scent of toast and bacon was in the air. The room was decorated in pink-and-black, jazz colours, and tall vases of gum leaves lent the air an outback scent.

It was modern and stylish without being so *outré* that it would be out of fashion in a year.

Miss Fisher was pleased to approve, and to load her plate with eggs and bacon and toast. Dot joined her, equally hungry, and they were drinking their second cup of tea before they had time to speak.

'You know that they've found the body, Dot?'

'Yes, Miss, that cop told me. How did she die?'

'I'd say a massive fracture of the skull, but she was extensively damaged, Dot, I hope and trust after she was dead. And her rings are missing—all those emeralds.'

'Robbery?' asked Dot.

'Murder, Dot. Robbery was probably an afterthought. No one would go to all that trouble just to rob an old woman, rings or no rings—at least, I don't think so. People are strange. Have some marmalade, it's excellent.'

'When do you reckon that cop will let us go?' asked Dot, taking some marmalade. Phryne was right—it was excellent.

'Have to be fairly soon, Dot, after all, they've found the body and none of us could have killed her…except me, of course. I wonder if he suspects me!'

'Suspects you, Miss!' Dot was indignant. 'You wouldn't go through all this mucking about if you wanted to kill someone. Like a play, this is, not like real life.'

'You are very acute, Dot. That is exactly what it is. Just like a play. Elaborate, theatrical and stagey. Hello! Here comes our policeman now. Who has he with him?'

Sergeant Wallace came into the breakfast-room, leading a girl by the hand. She was about twelve or thirteen, with two long plaits of brown hair and a skimpy, too-tight dress in shabby winceyette. She was carrying a battered leather attaché-case and a felt hat, the elastic of which was frayed by chewing. The sergeant led her over to Phryne's table and said:

'Well, Miss Fisher, Robbo said that you have a talent for mysteries, and here's one that I can't solve. This young woman was on the train, that's clear enough, for she had a ticket to Ballarat in her pocket, done up with a safety pin. She was found standing on the platform at Ballarat. No one came for her, and no one knows her, and she can't remember her own name. She can't tell us anything at all about herself, and I don't mind telling you I'm stumped. Perhaps you'd do me the favour of taking charge of her for the moment, until we can get the Welfare onto it?'

At the mention of the word 'Welfare', Dot had gone pale, and Phryne did not fail to notice this, feeling rather the same herself. In her childhood of straitened circumstances, the Welfare, who took children away so that they were never seen again, was a hideous phantom.

'No, no, there is no need to trouble them,' she said hastily, taking the girl's hand and sitting her down beside Dot. 'We will be delighted to look after the poor little mite, won't we, Dot?'

Dot nodded and went to fetch a fresh cup and a plate for the girl. The sergeant was about to leave when Phryne seized his arm.

'There's something I forgot to tell you,' she whispered. 'Her fingers were bare, weren't they? And when I saw her first, they were loaded down with rings—valuable ones—mostly emeralds and diamonds.'

'Thanks, Miss Fisher, that is a help. Robbery might be the motive, then, though I can't imagine how that advances matters. How is the daughter?'

'I left her sleeping peacefully. I'll send Dot to help her with her toilet as soon as she's finished breakfast. Dr. Heron had better see her again before she gets up, she was very deeply drugged.'

The sergeant agreed and went away. Phryne came back to her table to find that the girl had been helped to eggs and bacon and toast and tea and was eating as though she was famished.

'Slow down, old thing, there's plenty more,' she said, and the girl looked up, smiled, and laid down her knife and fork to take a gulp of tea.

Phryne let her eat in peace as she observed her. Neat table manners, someone had taught her well; and if she had plaited her own hair, she was a tidy creature. She could not help the winceyette dress, which had been made for someone less coltish and thinner, and Phryne resolved to get rid of that dress as soon as possible. Though she had not spoken, she had understood what Phryne had said. Therefore she spoke English, which was a help. There were permanent blue shadows under the eyes which spoke of childhood illness, but she seemed sturdy enough. The nails on the large well-formed hands were bitten to the quick.

The girl finished her breakfast, pushing back the plate with a satisfied sigh, and Phryne poured her some more tea.

'I'm Phryne Fisher, and this is Dorothy Williams. What's your name?' she asked quietly, and the girl's brow puckered.

'I can't remember!' she said, and began to cry.

Dot hastily supplied her with a handkerchief and a hug, and Phryne said quickly, 'Never mind. We'll call you Jane. Would you like to come and stay with me for a while, Jane?'

Jane stopped crying and nodded, drying her face. Phryne smiled.

'Good, that's settled. Now I have to go and talk to that nice policeman again, so why don't you find yourself something pleasant to pass the time. There are books and games on that shelf. Dot will help you. See you in an hour or so, Dot.'

Phryne slung her red coat around her shoulders, checked that cigarettes and money reposed in her pockets, and sauntered out into the chilly yard to find the sergeant.

She found him staring mournfully at the stable door, whence two well-dressed men were carrying a stretcher.

'Going for autopsy in Melbourne,' he said in answer to her question. 'I hope she was dead when all that happened.'

'So do I. And I haven't got far with the new puzzle, either.'

'No? She don't remember?'

'She don't. I have called her Jane. Was she definitely on that train?'

'Why, yes, Miss, she was seen on it, second carriage from the end. Second-class ticket, single. Nothing on her to identify her, so the Ballarat people shipped her back, thinking that the two mysteries must be connected.'

'That is not necessarily the case,' said Phryne. 'She could have nothing to do with it.'

'And that's true too,' agreed the sergeant, in deepest gloom. 'Well, they've taken the body away, and now I have to break it to Miss Henderson. Hang on a tick. It would come much better from a woman. I don't suppose that you…'

Phryne sighed. She had thought that this might happen.

'All right. I'll tell Miss Henderson if you take me to see the scene of the crime.'

'Deal,' agreed the sergeant, and Phryne returned to the hotel.

Miss Henderson was sitting up in bed and taking a little toast and tea when Miss Fisher arrived. Dot had taken the child Jane into the bathroom and was abjuring her to wash behind her ears. Miss Henderson took one look at Phryne's solemn face and said, 'Mother's dead, isn't she?'

'Yes, I'm afraid she is.'

'You know, I thought she must be.'

Miss Henderson began to cry, in a helpless way, seeming to be unaware that she was still holding a piece of toast in one hand and her cup of tea in the other. Phryne took away the cup and the toast and gave Miss Henderson a handkerchief, three of which she had prudently provided.

Miss Henderson wiped her face and leaned forward, grabbing Phryne's wrist in a fierce grip.

'You are a detective, are you not? I read about that case of the unspeakable little man you caught in Queenscliff. And the Spanish ambassador's son's kitten. You're clever. You can catch him for me.'

'Catch whom?' asked Phryne, fighting the urge to free her hand. 'Calm yourself, Miss Henderson.'

'The murderer, of course.'

'Do you really want to hire me? Think about it. I may find out the truth.'

'That's what I want you to find,' said Miss Henderson firmly. 'I know that Mother was a nuisance. I have quite often felt like killing her myself, God forgive me, but that does not mean that I did it or contrived it. Murder is such a monstrous thing. And why? Why? The person she injured most was me—hounding me, nagging me, day after day, hour after hour, until I thought I'd go mad! If anyone had reason to kill Mother, it was me, but I didn't. And now I don't know what to do or where to turn.'

She sobbed for a few minutes, then took control of herself again, putting down the handkerchief.

'So I want to hire you, Miss Fisher, to find whoever killed my mother. Find out the truth.'

'All right,' agreed Phryne, sitting down on the end of the bed. 'On condition that you drink the rest of that tea and don't get up until the doctor has seen you.'

'I'll be good. Miss Fisher, tell me—did she suffer?'

'No,' said Phryne, thinking of the great blow the old woman had taken to the head—surely no awareness could survive that. 'No, I'm sure she did not suffer.'

'How did she…die?'

'She was hit on the head very hard,' said Phryne. 'One heavy blow. But her body was much damaged after she was dead—the fall from the train, possibly.'

'Can I see her?'

'No, the body has gone to Melbourne for *post mortem*. You can see her later. She looks fine. Her face is quite untouched. She will not shock you.'

'She shocked me enough when she was alive,' commented Miss Henderson wryly. 'I doubt that she'll shock me that much now that she is dead.'

Phryne left Eunice Henderson to her tea and found Dot, who had Jane's clothes over her arm.

'Well, any name tags or laundry marks, Dot?'

'Nothing at all, Miss. I tell you one thing, she's a cleanly little madam, but she ain't used to a bath. She's been cat-washing since she was a baby, I reckon.'

Phryne recalled cat-washes, because she had taken them herself until the death of some young men had dragged her upwards into the world of running water and bathrooms. One obtained a bowl of hot water, and standing on a mat and removing one article of clothing at a time, one washed first face and hands, then the upper body, removing the shirt, then the lower body, removing and replacing the skirt, until finally one stood both feet in the basin (assuming that they would fit) having washed the whole person in about two pints of hot water, or one kettle-full. It was satisfying in an economical sort of way, but was nothing like the joyful sensation of sinking into a hot, scented bath. Phryne almost envied Jane the pleasure which she must be experiencing.

'What about the clothes themselves?'

'Hand-me-downs,' said Dot without hesitation. 'See—hem's been let down twice, and the colour's faded with a lot of washing. Homemade,' she added, exhibiting the inside collar where no label had ever been attached. 'And not very well, either. Her singlet and bloomers are wool, but old and scratchy, and thin enough to put your fingers through.'

'Well, she can't put those back on,' commented Phryne. 'Can you find something of mine that will fit?'

'No, Miss, I'll go out directly and buy her some suitable clothes,' said Dot, shocked that this waif should be clothed in Phryne's silk underwear. 'That would be better, Miss.' Phryne gave Dot enough money to purchase clothes to last Jane until she got back to Phryne's own house, and dragged herself away to find the sergeant yet again. He was still standing in the yard, gloomily smoking a cigarette and communing with the crows who were gathered on the milking shed fence.

'Well, I've told Miss Henderson and it's time for you to keep your part of the bargain,' she said brightly. The crows, alarmed by the extreme redness of her coat, rose flapping in a body, making raucous comments.

'Very well, Miss Fisher, I've got a car, come along. It's not far,' added the depressed sergeant. 'And blessed if I can see how she was got out. I've walked every inch of the line, both with a lantern and in daylight,' he said, helping Miss Fisher into the battered Model T and cranking the engine into a sputtering semblance of life. 'And there isn't a footprint or a mark of where she fell.'

Chapter Three

'So young a child,' said the gentleman sit-
ting opposite to her, (he was dressed in white
paper) 'ought to know which way she's going,
even if she doesn't know her own name!'

Alice Through the Looking Glass,
Lewis Carroll

'That's where they found the body,' said the sergeant as
they stood beside the track. 'A good ten yards. She can't have
fallen that far, and there is not a mark, Miss Fisher...look for
yourself.'

Phryne stepped away from the track and surveyed the ground.
The water tower with its wooden scaffolding stood about fifteen feet high, with the cloth funnel that fed the train hanging
down. The ground was firm but moist red clay, the consistency
of an ice-cream brick, and certainly there was no sign of anyone
walking on it. Further away, along the path, were the multiple
tracks of the searchers, the clay reproducing their bootmarks
and even the round indentation where someone had set down
a lantern, and the cup-shaped prints of knees next to the body.
There were multiple marks there, but the ground was all cut up,
churned and confused by the searchers so no individual print
could be discerned.

'She was trodden into the mud,' said the sergeant. 'They near had to dig her out. Over there, Miss Fisher, you can see.'

'Yes, what a mess! No chance of finding anything there. Have you walked along a bit further?'

'Yes, Miss, a good half mile, but this is where she landed, however she got out. A bit further back I found the glass where you broke your window, and that must mark the beginning of the whole thing. Before that, Mrs. Henderson was alive.'

'Hmm, yes. Has anyone climbed the water tower?'

'Yes, Miss, I thought of that, but the canvas funnel isn't long enough to catch, and the train-men were using it to refill the boiler. There's nothing unusual up there, Miss.'

'It was just a thought. Well, we might go back to Ballan, then, Sergeant, and have a look at the first-class carriage.'

'All right, Miss. Er...how did Miss Henderson take the news of her mother's death?'

'She was very distressed; not that I think that she liked her mother at all, indeed, the old lady was fretting the life out of her, but she has hired me to find out who killed her, and I don't think that she did it, I really don't.'

'Hired you, Miss? Will you take the assignment?'

'Oh, yes, I think so. I want to find the murderer too. I don't like having my journeys interrupted by chloroform.'

The Model T made the short journey to the rail siding without shedding any of the more essential of its parts, and they shuddered to a halt. A very large constable was on guard next to the train. He stood up hurriedly when he saw the sergeant and endeavoured to hide his doorstep cheese sandwich behind his back.

'Anyone been about, Jones?' asked the sergeant, elaborately not noticing the sandwich. 'All quiet?'

'Sir, that Mrs. Lilley came and collected some of the children's clothes, but I made sure that she only went into her compartment, sir.'

'And that's all?'

'Yes, sir.'

'All right. You can go and get some breakfast—take half an hour, you must be hungry.' The sergeant smiled laconically, and allowed Phryne to precede him onto the train.

'The smell's almost gone,' she commented. 'Thank goodness. Here's where I was sitting, and Dot. Nothing there. Here is the lair of those awful children. Mr. and Mrs. Cotton were here…tell me, has anything been touched?'

'No, Miss Fisher, except when Miss Henderson was removed. Why? Something missing?'

'The cloth, the one that was laid over her face. It isn't here. Perhaps they took it with Miss Henderson. Otherwise it looks just as it did. Now, see, Sergeant, look at these marks.' The sergeant came fully into the compartment, which had two long padded seats. Both ladies had evidently been reclining, almost or fully asleep. A woolly rug was flung from the seat nearest the engine and was crumpled on the floor. The shawl on the other seat was thrown to the end, as though the sleeper had arisen hurriedly.

'See, they were both lying here, heads to the outside wall, with the window open like that. At least I suppose the window was open. I must ask Miss Henderson. I heard her mother complaining about the window quite a lot, but she didn't seem to have a preference really. She was just doing it to irritate. "She only does it to annoy, because she knows it teases".'

The sergeant, who was evidently unfamiliar with *Alice in Wonderland*, looked blank.

'Then,' continued Phryne, bending close to the windowsill, 'see? Those scrape marks. She was pulled out the window after she was drugged—I hope—and…'

'And?' prompted the sergeant with heavy irony, 'carried up into the air by angels? Lifted up by aeroplane?'

'Yes, that is a problem, I agree, my dear police officer, but it's clear she was dragged. Look at the marks! Plain as the nose on your face.'

'Yes, that is what they look like, as though something has been pulled through that window, and even a little of her hair has caught, Miss, I believe you are right. But what happened then I can't imagine. She was thrown a long way, Miss.'

'What if the murderer were on the roof of the train?' asked Phryne suddenly. 'Has it rained since last night?'

'Well, yes, Miss, there was a shower at about five, quite a heavy one, that's why everything is so soggy.'

'Blast! That will have washed all the marks off the roof.'

'But you could have something there, Miss! If he was on the roof that would account for the marks, and even for where the body was found. She was a light little thing.'

'And the injuries?'

'Maybe the doctor was just indulging a diseased imagination. Not much happens in Ballan, you know.'

'So she could have been that damaged by such a fall?'

'I reckon so, Miss. That train builds up speed. She'd hit the earth with a fair old thump.'

'Well, there's not much else to see in here,' commented Phryne, noting that the old lady had a lurid taste in reading matter. Next to her place was an edition of *Varney the Vampire* which Phryne remembered from her youth to be fairly blood-chilling. Miss Henderson had been beguiling the journey with *Manon Lescaut*, in French, the unexpurgated edition. By the bookmark she had nearly finished it. Phryne reflected that the woman who chose *Manon* and the woman who preferred *Varney* were hardly likely to be soul mates.

Most of the hand-baggage had been taken to the hotel, but Phryne picked up one parcel which seemed to contain paper and was addressed to Miss Henderson. She weighed it in her hands and put it down again—just paper.

The sergeant escorted her out of the train to the hotel. The constable was returning from what, to judge from the crumbs which he was brushing off his uniform, had been a very good breakfast.

'Keep watch for a bit longer, lad,' said the sergeant, and looked hungrily toward the kitchen. Phryne interpreted the glance correctly.

'Good heavens, man, have you not eaten? You can't deduce things on an empty stomach. Mrs. Johnson makes an excellent omelette,' she added, and gave him a push.

She then walked back to her own room to see if Dot had extracted any information from the unknown girl.

She had been comprehensively washed and was enduring a punitive combing of her long hair, and bearing it pretty well, it seemed. Dot had obtained a very plain skirt and blouse in a depressing serge dyed with what appeared to be bitumen, but even in these unpromising clothes the girl was rather pretty.

As Phryne entered, the hair was at last drawn back from her face and Jane sat up and sighed with relief.

'I always hated having my hair dressed,' commented Phryne. 'That's why I cut it short as soon as I could. How do you feel, Jane?'

'Very well, Miss,' said Jane calmly. 'But I still can't remember anything. It's like there's a hole in my memory. As though I was just born.'

'Hmm. There are several things about you that we know. One is that you are an Australian; the accent is unmistakable. You speak English. And there are things that you have not forgotten: how to eat with a knife and fork, how to read, how to converse. I therefore conclude that you will get your memory back in time if you don't worry at it.'

Jane looked relieved. Phryne left her to play a quiet game of solitaire, which she also remembered, it seemed, and drew Dot aside.

'Dot, those clothes!'

'Yes, Miss, I know, but that's all they had in the general store, and I had to dress her in something. You would have liked the other clothes even less than these. They don't have no style in the outback,' said Dot, to whom all places more than four miles from the GPO were country. Phryne smiled and forebore to comment.

'Never mind, they will last her until we get back to the city. How does she strike you?'

'I reckon that she is telling the truth,' said Dot twisting her plait. 'Every time she tries to think about who she is she starts to tremble and to sweat, and you can't fake that. Why she can't remember is more than I can tell. She's healthy, though skinny, and I reckon she's about thirteen. There's no bruise or mark on her and I couldn't find a lump on her head. Her eyes are clear so I don't think that she's been drugged.'

'If we can rule out trauma and drugs then I think it has to be shock, and that is something that wears off, it can't be broken through. Like Mary's Little Lamb, we leave her alone and she'll come home, bringing her tail behind her. Meanwhile the mystery deepens. I can't imagine how Mrs. Henderson was got out of the train—at least, she was dragged out of the window, but all the signs seem to indicate that she was dragged up, and unless the murderer was on the roof of the train, I don't know how that can be. Any ideas, Dot?'

'No, Miss, not at the moment.'

'Very well, let's have a brief chat with the others who were on the train and then I think that we shall go back to Melbourne. There's nothing more to do here and somehow I've gone right off trains, and Ballarat, too.'

'Me, too,' agreed Dot. 'Next time, can we take the car, Miss?'

Phryne smiled. At last, her nervous maid had been converted to the joys of motoring. But it had taken a murder to convince her.

The surviving passengers were all grouped in the pink and black breakfast-room. The pregnant woman looked washed-out and leaned on a husband who had lost all of his bounce. Mrs. Lilley's appalling children had been stuffed with so many sweets and cakes by a distracted mother and a sympathetic cook that they sat, bloated and queasy, quiet for the moment. Miss Henderson had risen and dressed and was the calmest of the group. The burns had blistered during the night and she was obviously in pain. Mrs. Johnson had served tea and coffee and Miss Henderson was sipping milk through a straw.

Phryne took her seat and accepted a cup of coffee from the hovering landlady.

Sergeant Wallace came in, a massive presence which seemed to fill the doorway, and everyone looked up, falling silent. He raised a hand, embarrassed.

'Nothing new, ladies and gentlemen, but a couple more questions and then you can go on, or go back, whatever suits you. First: did anyone notice a young guard?'

Mrs. Lilley looked up.

'Yes, a blond young man, rather good looking? He passed me twice. The first time he stopped and said hello, then the next time that I saw him he seemed to be avoiding me, but I didn't think anything of it.'

'Why not, if he was pleasant the first time?'

'Johnnie bit him,' admitted Mrs. Lilley shamefacedly. 'He was being a dog and the young man wouldn't pat him, so he bit him—I don't know why my children aren't like anyone else's!—so after that, of course, I wasn't surprised that he didn't want to talk to us again. It would be different if my husband hadn't died,' said poor Mrs. Lilley. 'And he had shell-shock so he couldn't discipline them. But oh, dear, I wish I had stayed home!'

Mrs. Lilley burst into tears. The children, shocked, clustered around her and patted her, Johnnie delivering a fierce hack to the ankle of Sergeant Wallace, whom he perceived as a persecutor of his mother. The sergeant, to his credit, winced in silence and merely held the child in a tight but comforting grip.

'You take a hold of yourself, young feller-me-lad,' he admonished. 'You be nice to your mum, now, and don't drive her mad with all your pranks. Mrs. J, perhaps you could come up with some sal volatile. Anyone else see this guard?'

Mr. and Mrs. Cotton shook their heads. They had been involved, it seemed, in an engrossing quarrel over whose duty it was to lock the back door, and this had kept them going until they had both fallen asleep. They had not noticed the young guard.

Mrs. Johnson had produced the sal volatile and Mrs. Lilley appeared to be recovering. She was, it appeared, taking her little demons to her relatives in Ballarat, and Phryne fervently hoped that they were prepared for the invasion.

'Now, if you will all give me your names and addresses and a telephone number if you have one, you can all be on your way. I've hired the station taxi to take all the stuff and the Ballarat train will be through in an hour.'

'Miss Fisher, can I ask you a question?' asked Mr. Cotton. 'Did you see this guard? And do you think that he was the murderer?'

'Yes, I saw him, and I think he might have been the murderer,' answered Phryne carefully. 'And I have a question for you. Has anyone seen this girl before?'

She nodded toward the door, where Dot was escorting Jane into the room. All the passengers looked at her narrowly, and she blushed and hung her head.

'I call her Jane,' said Phryne, making a broad gesture. 'She can't remember who she is. Can anyone help?'

The Cottons shook their heads. Mrs. Lilley looked up from her sal volatile to sigh. Little Johnnie, however, gave a whoop of joy and ran forward to embrace as much of Jane as he could reach, which was about knee-level. Jane's face lit up, and she lifted the child and embraced him.

'Johnnie!' she cried. 'Your name is Johnnie!' Then the young brow clouded, and she bent her head, as though the weight of her hair pulled it down. 'But I don't know any more,' she mourned.

'Mrs. Lilley, did your children leave the first-class carriage?' asked Phryne.

Mrs. Lilley shrugged.

'They were running around all over the place, dear, for quite a while, especially when I was changing the baby. I lost Johnnie for quite half an hour, I believe, when we got onto the train. I don't know where he was, it was dark, and I was worried, but he turned up as good as gold, like he always does, bless him. He might have got out of the carriage. I'll ask him.'

'Johnnie,' she began in a calm voice. 'Tell Mummy where you met the girl.'

Johnnie, clinging tight to Jane, shook his head and shut his mouth tight.

'Johnnie, Mummy won't be angry if you went out of the carriage. Tell me, where did you meet the girl?'

Johnnie unlocked his lips long enough to say, 'No,' firmly.

'I'll give you this cake if you tell me,' bribed Phryne, and Johnnie repeated, 'No,' in a deeply regretful tone. 'Has someone told you not to tell?' persisted Phryne, and Johnnie nodded. 'A man in a uniform?' asked the sergeant, and Johnnie nodded again. 'Well, I'm a policeman, and you always have to tell policemen the truth, you know that, don't you?' Johnnie nodded again.

'Well, where did you meet the girl?' asked Sergeant Wallace, and Johnnie said, 'Dark,' and grabbed for the cake.

Phryne swung it up out of grasping distance and said, 'Dark where?'

'Paddock,' said Johnnie. 'Train stop. In paddock. She put Johnnie back on train. Chuff, chuff, chuff,' he commented. 'Cake now.'

Phryne gave him his cake. She felt that he had earned it. But the puzzle had become worse.

'Cryptic infant,' she commented as Johnnie ate about half of the chocolate cake and smeared the rest evenly over his countenance. 'What do you think he meant, Mrs. Lilley?'

'Oh dear, Miss Fisher, he's such a clever little boy, there's no telling what he meant—I mean, he may be telling the truth, but he does make things up, I'm afraid.'

'What sort of things does he make up?' asked Phryne. Mrs. Lilley blushed.

'Well, he said that there was a bear under his bed, and there simply isn't room,' she added, sounding imbecilic even to her own ears. 'And he said that his father came and tucked him in and said good night, when his father has been dead for eight months.'

'Did so,' affirmed Johnnie. 'Daddy came. Scared away the bear. More cake?' he asked, with an unexpectedly charming smile.

'Well, perhaps his father did come back to the precious pet,' commented Dot, unexpectedly maternal. Johnnie turned his face confidingly up to Jane.

'Girl in the dark,' he reiterated, as this had yielded cake before. 'In the paddock. Outside the train. Johnnie climb down. Girl lift me up. Johnnie was scared.'

'Of the bear?' asked the policeman, gently. Johnnie blushed, resembling his mother for the first time.

'Bears in the dark,' he agreed. 'Girl put Johnnie back in the light. No bears. Nice girl. Johnnie likes girl. Down now,' he requested, and Jane put him on his feet. He ran to his mother and buried his face in her skirt.

'Jane, you must have got off the train for some reason, found Johnnie there, and put him back, that's what he means by "into the light", I expect. Does any of that ring a bell?'

For a moment the girl's face had an intense, concentrated look, as if she were listening to a distant sound, but it died away. She shook her head.

'Never mind—it will come. Now, who's coming back to Melbourne with me? Miss Henderson?'

Miss Henderson looked pained.

'I would be grateful for the company,' she said with difficulty. 'Mother and I have a house, you know, but it is all shut up for the winter.'

'Good. The Melbourne train is in half an hour. Dot will help you to pack. Is there an account to pay, Mrs. Johnson?'

'No, Miss Fisher, the Railways is taking care of all that.'

'Good. Here is my card. If you recall anything that might help, then please call me on this telephone number.'

She distributed a number of her own cards: 'Miss Phryne Fisher. Investigations. 221B, The Esplanade, St. Kilda'.

She had reached the door and was leaving when she remembered something, and beckoned to the sergeant. He joined her.

'Did you find the cloth?'

'The one with the chloroform? Yes, Miss. It's in the station. Want to walk over there with me?'

Phryne laid one hand on his arm and he escorted her down the street to the small wooden building that housed the police station. It was bare but tidy, with ledger and telephone and desk.

The sergeant produced a cardboard box, from which emanated a strong stench of chloroform. He held it out. Quickly, holding her breath, Phryne shook out a strip of common white pineapple towelling, such as is supplied in public toilets and at cheap hotels. It had a faint blue thread running through it that indicated that it had belonged to someone who had their laundry commercially done.

'Cheap and nasty, and he hasn't even used the whole towel,' she commented, handing the rag back. 'I think that shows a really unpleasant form of economy. Nothing there, Sergeant. Are you going to keep this case, or will it go to CID in Melbourne?'

'Probably to CID, Miss, which is a pity. I would have looked forward to working with you,' he said, greatly daring, and Phryne took his face between her hands and kissed him soundly.

'I would have liked that too, my dear Sergeant Wallace, but I'm afraid that I must love you and leave you. Farewell,' she breezed and left to catch the train to Melbourne, abandoning a deeply impressed policeman without a backward glance.

'If she's a flapper,' mused the sergeant, wiping Passionate Rouge lipstick off his blameless mouth, 'then I'm all for 'em, and I don't care what Mum says.'

Chapter Four

'She'll have to go back from here as luggage!'
Alice Through the Looking Glass,
Lewis Carroll

Phryne caught the train with seconds to spare, as Johnnie had seriously objected to parting with Jane, and had to be placated with yet more cake. Dot, with customary efficiency, had loaded all Phryne's belongings, Miss Henderson, Jane, and herself aboard ten minutes before, and was in a fever lest Phryne should miss this train and have to wait for the next, which was a slow one, stopping at all the intervening stations. Miss Henderson smiled wryly through her blisters and remarked, 'She must be a sore trial to you.'

Dot immediately bridled. No one criticized Phryne in front of her and got away with it.

'She's the dearest, sweetest, cleverest mistress any woman could get,' she declared. 'She's only late because she's stopped to soothe that crying child. She's been very good to me and I won't hear a word against her.'

'My apologies,' muttered Miss Henderson, rather taken aback. 'I did not mean any insult.'

Before Dot could reply, Phryne herself came running, flung herself aboard the train, and sat down panting.

'Whew!' She fanned herself. 'I thought I'd never bribe that small monster to silence. He's going to be as fat as a little pig if someone doesn't take him in hand.'

The train started with a jerk, and Phryne found the novel which she had been reading, and handed to Miss Henderson her copy of *Manon Lescaut*. She accepted the book, nodded her thanks, and opened it. The carriage was silent all the way to Melbourne.

◇◇◇

Phryne had telephoned ahead, and Mr. Butler was at the station to meet them. Phryne's houseman was proudly at the wheel of the massive and elegant fire-engine red Hispano-Suiza, Phryne's prize possession. Even she did not like to think of what she had paid for it, but it was worth every penny. The coachwork, applied by a master, had been lovingly polished, and all the brass and chrome glittered in the still, cold air. Jane drew in an audible breath at the sight of the magnificent car.

'Is it not lovely?' asked Phryne dotingly, as Mr. Butler climbed out to pile the luggage in the back, and to seat the ladies. Jane nodded, awed. Even Miss Henderson seemed impressed.

'Soon be home, ladies,' said Mr. Butler bracingly. 'Mrs. Butler has a nice small luncheon on the stove and your rooms are all ready. Nice cup of tea as soon as you get in,' he added, as he was convinced that the cure for almost all feminine woes was a nice cup of tea.

'I've rung Dr. MacMillan as you asked, Miss,' he said in an undertone to Phryne, who had seated herself in the front seat, consenting to be driven for this time. 'She'll be along directly, she says, and she can come to lunch.'

'Very good, Mr. B., you've done well. Sorry to land back on your hands after promising to be away for a week,' she said, and Mr. Butler grinned as he started the big car and moved away from the kerb.

'Oh, that's all right, Miss. It's too quiet without you around.'

'You know that we have had a murder?' she asked, and the grey head nodded, his eyes on the road.

'Yes, Miss, them newspaper reporters were around this morning, looking for a story. I told 'em you weren't here, and they slunk away, but they'll be back, though perhaps not tonight. It's in all the papers, Miss. I've bought 'em, as I thought you'd like to see 'em.'

'Excellent. Quite right. But we might keep them away from Miss Henderson. It was her mother, you know.'

Mr. Butler whistled.

'They're up in your sitting room, Miss,' he said. 'Mrs. B. thought as how you might be bringing the poor lady home.'

They arrived at Phryne's bijou residence somewhat shaken and partially frozen, and did not see much of the house as they were ushered inside to a blazing log fire and the cheering scent of hot buttered muffins, cinnamon toast, and pot pourri, of which Phryne was very fond. She had two big Chinese bronze bowls, encircled with dragons, and these were filled with rose leaves and petals, verbena and orris root. Beside the fireplace was a tall famille rose jar filled with wintersweet.

'Come in, my dears, and sit down,' said Phryne solicitously, ushering her guests into the salon and taking their coats.

'A bitter day for tragedy and train journeys! Mrs. B. will have some tea made instantly. Sit down, Jane, warm your hands. Miss Henderson, perhaps you'd like to lie down.'

'No, dear, I would hate to miss this fire. What a quantity of wood. And what a heat! Oh, I do love a fire. It makes even winter bearable.'

This was the first sign of enthusiasm which Phryne had seen from Miss Henderson, and it seemed genuine. Mr. Butler, having helped the ailing lady into the house, went out to park the car and assist the boy in bringing in more wood for the house. Miss Fisher was not afraid of expense in a reasonable cause and she had purchased a pyramid sized heap of dry, split wood.

The seating provided was in the form of large, overstuffed leather armchairs and a big club settee, drawn close to the fire. The overwhelming blues and greens of the room were set off by the red light. Phryne had dropped her red mantle and kicked off her shoes, flinging herself into one of the armchairs and holding out her frozen feet to the flames.

'Gosh, I think that all my toes would have dropped off if that ride had lasted another ten minutes. Ah. Tea,' she added with deep appreciation, as Mrs. Butler brought in the trolley loaded with the big silver tea pot and further plates of goodies. A glass of brandy and milk had been provided for Miss Henderson, and she sipped it decorously through a straw.

Jane took a cup of tea, added three sugars and a lot of milk, and was given a plate and free range among the edibles. Restraining a small cry of delight, which Phryne found very touching, she took a wedge of toast and a muffin to begin with.

A ring at the doorbell announced Dr. MacMillan. She bustled in, shaking water off her rough tweed coat, and was provided with tea and muffins.

'Oh, Lord, what a nasty day!' she exclaimed. 'Cold as a Monday morning in Manchester, so it is.'

'Miss Henderson, Jane, this is Dr. MacMillan, an old friend of mine. I've asked her here to have tea, and also to take a look at you both, because I am rather worried about your condition. Miss Henderson has been chloroformed, and Jane can't remember who she is.'

'Well!' The patients surveyed the doctor as she looked them up and down. Dr. MacMillan was a stout, ruddy woman of fifty, vigorous and brave, with pepper and salt hair and a weather-ruined complexion. She was dressed in a tweed gentleman's suit with formal white shirt, collar, tie, and waistcoat, and she had large, capable hands, now cradling the tea-cup. She saw a thin, frightened girl with long plaits and a bluish cast to a pale countenance, and a stately and well-dressed, intelligent woman with a burnt face, calmly sipping her drink. The doctor finished her tea and muffin and slapped down the cup.

'You first, my bird,' she said to Jane and gave her an encouraging grin. 'Lost your memory, eh? There have been times, ay there have, when I've wished that I had the losing of mine. The front room, Phryne?'

'Yes, it's all ready,' answered Phryne. Dr. MacMillan escorted Jane out.

She was back in a quarter of an hour, and Jane was, it seemed, rather relieved than otherwise by the examination. Miss Henderson arose and crossed the room under her own power, and the doctor closed the door again.

'More tea, Jane? What did Dr. MacMillan say?'

'She said there's nothing wrong with me that time won't cure, and that I should drink lots of milk and sleep and my memory will come back. Isn't she lovely?' asked Jane in a hero-worshipping trance. 'Could I be a doctor, I wonder? Not a nurse, but a doctor—like Dr. MacMillan?'

'I don't see why not, but it depends on how hard you study,' said Phryne. 'We've got it easy, compared to Dr. MacMillan. She had to fight the whole medical establishment to become a doctor—in her day they wouldn't allow women interns into the wards, in case they should see something which would shock their delicacy.'

'I think…I think I'm quite good at school,' faltered Jane.

Phryne scanned the bookshelves and gathered an armload of texts.

'Here, take one of these in turn and read aloud,' she instructed, and Jane opened *Origin of Species* and began to read with some fluency. Phryne was impressed. When the girl reached *Alice in Wonderland*, she flushed, and dropped the book.

'I've read this before,' she exclaimed. 'But I can't recall how it ends.'

'Jane, I have a high opinion of your brains. If you never get your memory back, it does not matter. If we can't find your family, I will send you to university if you want to become a doctor. So don't worry. I don't care if you never remember. Why not read the rest of Alice and see how it comes out?' Phryne left Jane lying on the hearthrug, eating cinnamon toast and dripping happy tears onto *Tractatus Philosophicus*.

'Dry old tome, anyway,' muttered Phryne, and went to find Dot.

Phryne had renovated her house extensively, and one thing of which she was rather proud was the conversion of a dull sitting-room on the ground floor back into two neat little guest rooms. Both had electric fires, and one still had the original grate. Phryne had allotted this one to Miss Henderson as soon as she had observed that lady's love affair with fire. The rooms had been washed a pale peach, with bright curtains and bedspread in one and furnishings of a deep and soothing green in the other. Phryne hoped that Jane, who seemed to be a studious child, would not object to the grass-green, pink and black stripes which wriggled across her bed.

She made a brief check for clean towels and new soap, although she was sure that Mrs. Butler would not have tolerated a fold out of place. She was correct. Everything was in order and a small but hot fire burned in the grate in the peach and green room.

The door opened, and Mr. Butler entered, carrying Miss Henderson with apparent effort, and Dr. MacMillan turned back the bed.

'Find her a nightdress, Phryne, the poor woman's worn out with shock and pain. Thank you, Mr. Butler,' she added, and that invaluable man left the room. 'I've written a prescription for a cocaine ointment which should help. There's nothing more consistently painful than a burn, and I've given her some Chloral so she should sleep for a few hours. By then she will be feeling better, I think, but she should keep to her bed for at least a week. Are you prepared to keep her, Phryne?'

'Certainly, poor woman, she can't go home to a bare house and no care. We can look after her, Dot and me. What should we look out for?'

'I'll come each day to dress her face, we must be careful that she does not break the blisters by scratching, or she may have a scar. Otherwise she will be sleepy and sad, and will need a warm bed, plenty of liquids, and light nourishing food, which I dare say your admirable Mrs. Butler can manage. There, I'll just tuck her in, and we'll leave her alone. Is that fire safe?'

Phryne accompanied the doctor back to the sitting-room, where Jane had mopped her tears hastily and was now studying Glaister on Poisons. Dr. MacMillan observed this with pleasure.

'You're a keen study,' she commented. 'But you'd better read *Alice* while you have the chance.'

'Have you read *Alice in Wonderland?*' asked Jane, astonished, and Dr. MacMillan laughed comfortably and took a scone.

'Certainly I have, and recently, too. A fine book to keep your perspective.' She bit into the scone. 'Child, could you go into the kitchen and ask for some more tea? I'm parched with all this work.'

Jane went out, delighted to do something to help. Dr. MacMillan laid an urgent hand on Phryne's shoulder.

'You must keep that child safe,' she whispered, spattering Phryne with crumbs. 'She's been molested, and I fear that is why she lost her memory.'

'Raped?' asked Phryne, turning sick.

'No. Mishandled, however, and attempted, I'd say, and not too long ago. Maybe a week.'

'I'll keep her as my own rather than let anything like that happen to the poor little thing.'

'Good. That is what I hoped to hear.'

'But what if she recovers her memory?'

'You must find the man,' said Dr. MacMillan. 'I think she may have come from an orphanage. They send their girls out when they are twelve or thirteen, and rape or worse is the fate of many of them. Perhaps she should be photographed. Someone should remember her.'

Jane came back with more tea, and they read *Alice in Wonderland* aloud until it was time for a brisk walk before dinner.

Chapter Five

*'I was very nearly putting you out of the
window into the snow! And you'd have
deserved it, you little mischievous darling!...now you can't deny it, kitty!'*

Alice Through the Looking Glass,
Lewis Carroll

Five hours of sleep, and Miss Henderson awoke in pain and in
fear, gasping for air.

'Where am I?' she whispered, and someone leaned over and
turned up the bedside light. Dot helped Miss Henderson to sit
up against her arm and found the little jar which Dr. MacMillan
had instructed the pharmacist to compound.

'Don't you try and talk yet, Miss, until I can put some of this
stuff on your mouth. Doctor says that it might make your face
a bit numb but that'll be an improvement, eh?'

Dot smeared the cocaine ointment freely over the burns, using
the little spatula supplied for the purpose, and then helped her
patient to a drink.

'There, that's better, isn't it? You're in the Hon. Phryne Fisher's
house, and I'm Dot.'

Dot wondered fleetingly if Miss Henderson, too, was losing her memory, but this did not appear to be the case. The woman swallowed the barley water and smiled crookedly.

'Yes, of course I remember, how nice this all is! What a lovely room, and a fire and all. And that is my favourite shade of peach.' Miss Henderson took a little more of the cooling drink. 'I can sit up on my own, really.'

'All right, Miss, is there anything I can get you? Are you hungry?'

'Why,' said Miss Henderson, 'I believe that I am hungry. Indeed, I don't think I have had anything to eat for ever so long. Can you fetch me something?'

'Yes, Miss. How about a nice omelette, now? A little toast?'

'That would be lovely,' sighed Miss Henderson, relaxing into a pile of feather pillows—in all her life she had never had more than one pillow, as her mother had considered it unhealthy—and smiling a creditable smile.

Dot obtained an omelette and Mrs. Butler set the tray daintily, including a napkin in a ring and a vase of flowers.

'She'll likely be overset, poor thing, with her mother killed and all that, not to mention being hurt,' she fussed. 'Don't you drop that tray, now, Dot!'

'I'll be careful,' promised Dot, and carried it steadily. She watched her patient eat, removed the plate, and brought in a small cup of custard and a pot of tea.

'I did not mean to insult you when I said that Miss Fisher must be a trial,' explained Miss Henderson. 'I was very fond of my mother, and she was a trial. How old do you think I am?' she went on, and Dot shook her head.

'It's hard to tell with all them burns, Miss. You sound young.'

'So I am. I am twenty-seven. Younger, I guess, than your Miss Fisher, but Mother was convinced that I would never marry. "You'll be with me until I die, Eunice," she used to say—and now it's true, poor Mother, though she never meant it like that. She was furious when Alastair came on the scene and wanted to marry me, and she did her best to get rid of him, but he proved to be of sterner stuff than the rest. She told him that she knew that he was marrying me for my money, and he just smiled and agreed with her.'

'So you've got money, Miss?'

'Oh, a modest competance. It yields me three hundred a year, and the house is mine now.'

'More tea, Miss? Do you want me to call this Alastair, then? We are on the telephone.'

'He must be frantic,' gasped Miss Henderson, her hand flying to her mouth. 'And he wouldn't know where I am! Oh, lord, Dot, please, can you call him at his rooms, and tell him that I am quite safe and he can visit me? How could I have forgotten?'

'It's been a tiring day, Miss,' said Dot, writing down the telephone number. 'I'll ring him, Miss, don't you worry. You all right to be left? I'll do it now.'

'Yes, yes, please do it now,' begged Miss Henderson, and Dot went out and closed the door.

Dot conveyed the message through the medium of a phone which appeared to be in a fish-and-chip shop somewhere in Lygon Street, Carlton. A young man's voice came on the phone, breathless.

'Hello, hello? Damn this instrument! Hello? Are you there?'

'This is Miss Williams. I am calling for Miss Henderson,' repeated Dot patiently for the fourth time. 'Are you Mr. Thompson?'

'Yes, Alastair Thompson here, Miss Williams, where is Eunice?'

'Take down the address,' said Dot. '221B, The Esplanade, St. Kilda. Call tomorrow about three.'

'Is she all right?' bellowed the voice. Someone in the background was shrieking in Italian.

'She's burned her face with that chloroform and she's upset about her mother. Come at three,' yelled Dot and hung up.

Phryne had largely cured her of her dread of telephones but she still thought them a clumsy means of exchanging ideas. She went back to Miss Henderson and advised that the young man would call the next day, and Miss Henderson looked even more alarmed.

'I can't let him see me like this!' she wailed.

Phryne, having finished dinner, walked in at this point and heard the whole story in three minutes.

'Simple, my dear, you shall have a veil. Perfectly proper and it will stop you from alarming your young man. What does he do, Miss Henderson?'

'Please call me Eunice. He's in final year Medicine, he will be on the wards next year. He's twenty-five,' she said simply, 'and he wants to marry me.'

'Very nice,' said Phryne. 'Here's your medicine, Eunice. Drink it up like a good girl and I'll see you in the morning. How do you feel?'

Eunice patted the pillow, luxuriating in more comfort than she had ever enjoyed and shocked at herself for being so pleased.

'I feel fine,' she sighed, swallowed her Chloral Hydrate (which tasted foul) and fell instantly asleep.

Dot allowed Phryne to drag her into the sitting-room.

'Come into my parlour,' said Phryne, grinning wolvishly. 'And tell all. Who is this young man?'

'He's her intended, Miss, and her mother didn't like him. That's all I know about it. Give over pulling me, Miss, I didn't get no more out of her, except that she seems to have had a fair old time with her mum. Not a nice old lady, Miss.'

'No, she wasn't. However, the plot thickens. I shall be delighted to meet this excellent young man. Care to play a game of cards, Dot? It appears that our Jane also remembers how to play chess, though she won't beat Dr. MacMillan.'

'No, thanks, Miss, I want to have a bath and go to bed. It's been a long day and I think I've a cold coming on.'

'Poor Dot! Get Mrs. B. to make you a whisky toddy, and take a really hot bath. I shall read, then—there's a new novel I haven't even glanced at, the bookshop really is hopeless—I don't even recall ordering it.'

Dot climbed the stairs to her bathroom with her whisky toddy steaming in her hand. The last she saw of Phryne for the night was her concentrated, Dutch doll face bent over a book. But it was not the latest novel. It was Glaister, on Poisons.

◇◇◇

Jane slept soundly for about three hours, and then awoke to hear a small, odd sound. She lay frozen, gripped by a fear which was all the worse because she could not tell why she should be afraid. Something was scratching at the window. Jane, trembling, was in such an agony of fear that she could not bear to lie still any longer. She threw back the quilt and put her feet to the carpet, hoping that the bed would not creak. It creaked. She froze again. The room was as cold as ice. Nothing happened. Then the scratch came again, and an odd sound like an unoiled hinge. Was someone trying to open the window? That was too much. She leapt at the window and snatched back the curtain, unlocking the latch and thrusting at the frame. The window grated open with a gush of cold sleet and something small, cold, and black half-fell into Jane's lap. She shut the window again and locked it, cradling the creature in her arms. It was a kitten, perhaps six weeks old, thin as a little bag of bones and almost as cold as the weather. Jane clutched it to her bosom, shivering and laughing under her breath.

'Oh, kitty, you gave me such a fright! You're as cold as ice. Come on, kitty, you can come back to bed with me, and then we shall both be warm.'

Still trembling, Jane carried the icy bundle of wet fur back to her brightly patterned bed with the peach sheets, the Onkaparinga blankets, and the quilt and replaced herself in the small hollow in which she had formerly lain.

The kitten, warming into life, began to wash itself with precise licks, curled under the blankets, nestling under Jane's chin. It was an unobservant animal, or it might have wondered why its rescuer cried herself to sleep.

◇◇◇

Miss Eunice Henderson, tended by Dot, was washed and breakfasted by the time Phryne came in with a selection of veils and an armload of nightgowns.

'That's a perfectly sensible gown you've got on, Eunice, but you will need a change. Perhaps you'd like to borrow some of mine? And I've brought a few hats. We should be able to cobble something together.'

Eunice touched the fabrics reverently. Crêpe de Chine, silk, satin, all the luscious delicacy and flowing draperies of a whole harem-full of houris. Eunice tried to imagine herself in one of these extravagant garments and utterly failed.

'I can't wear any of these beautiful things, really, Phryne, I just wouldn't look right in them.'

'Oh, yes you would, you have a lovely figure—do you swim?—long legs and a swan neck. Something with a high neck, I think, to show off that jaw line, especially since we are going to conceal your face. What about this?'

She exhibited a satin robe and gown, cut in a rather medieval line, with high neck and flowing sleeves. They were edged in white rabbit fur, and were of a deep, mossy green.

'They are beautiful,' said Eunice. 'All right, I will borrow them if you don't mind.'

'Of course I don't mind, old dear. Now what about this hat? It matches the gown, and it has a nice long chin-veil.'

The hat was a Paris model, made by a *couturière* who actually liked women, and it was small and plain, but superbly made. In the gown and the hat, Eunice Henderson was astonished at how…well…really…how beautiful she looked. So was Phryne, who had not expected such an excellent result.

'You really do look smashing, Eunice. I think you should stay in bed,' said Phryne. 'Dr. MacMillan said so, and I have a great deal of respect for her opinions. Wait until she has dressed your face, and then we shall don the glad rags for your young man. Good morning, Jane. What have you got?' Jane entered, still clad in the bitumen serge, and carrying something small and alive. She held it out to Phryne.

'He came to my window last night. Can I keep him? Mrs. Butler said that she needs a cat to keep down the mice, and he won't eat much. Please.'

'Of course you can keep him, Jane. He actually came to you? That is a great compliment.' She took the kitten, which was so light that she feared it might float away. 'If Mrs. B. will have a cat, then he can stay. Take him out to the kitchen and give him a lot of food. Poor little creature is all skin and bone.' The kitten, which Phryne had been stroking, purred and gave her thumb a quick lick, then walked off her hand onto Jane's shoulder, where he perched, holding onto the plait and balancing with his absurd scrap of a tail.

'Isn't he a pretty one,' commented Miss Henderson. Jane beamed.

'He will need a bath and a collar,' said Phryne. 'We will buy one this morning in town. We are going to get you some clothes, for I cannot stand that dreadful suit a moment longer. Mrs. B. will look after the kitten. Have you given him a name?' Jane paused at the door, the familiar listening look on her face.

'I think he should be called Ember,' she said, and vanished in the direction of the washing up and the milk delivery, in both of which Ember took a deep professional interest.

'She's coming along,' commented Miss Henderson. 'Poor child. Still, she's fallen on her feet, finding you. As have I. There must be some cat in my family after all.'

◇◇◇

Phryne left Dot and Mrs. Butler to look after Eunice Henderson, and spent an interesting morning in the shops with Jane. The girl had good, if restrained taste, and seemed to prefer grey and dark blue, which certainly set off her brown-blonde hair and her brown eyes. Phryne bought two suits, shoes and stockings, and sufficient underwear and shirts for a week's wear. Phryne's laundry was sent to the Chinese every week. She laughed when Phryne suggested donating her black suit to the poor, and was still chuckling when Phryne stuffed the offending garments into the hands of a woman begging on the street corner near the station.

'See, that earned us a blessing,' said Phryne. 'Giving things away is a good way of acquiring merit, and not too hard on the purse. Here's our train, now, have we got everything?' She checked over the parcels. The collar and the flea-soap for Ember; the chrysanthemums, the unspoilt product of a hothouse, for Dot, who doted on them; the small vial of expensive 'Lalla' perfume and a box of 'Rachel *poudré riz*' for Phryne; the suitcase and all the rest of the clothes were to be sent on by the shops.

'Yes, that's everything, and here's the train.'

They found a corner seat and Phryne talked amiably with the girl all the way home, reflecting that good clothes make a great difference to an adolescent. Her gawkiness had been concealed by fine tailoring, and now she was such a refreshing sight that an elderly gentleman opposite them could not take his eyes off her all the way to St. Kilda, and on their way out of the train offered Phryne compliments on her sister.

Phryne laughed, linked arms with Jane, and walked along the sea front. The wind was cold but Jane was warm inside her new woollen topcoat, and her new shoes hardly hurt her feet at all.

'Miss Fisher?' asked Jane, tugging at Phryne's arm.

'Mmm?'

'Why are you doing all this for me?'

'What? For you? Well, there are several reasons. Because that nice policeman asked me to mind you. Because I would not hand a dog over to the Welfare. Because you are a mystery and mysteries interest me. Because you are intelligent and I am interested in establishing a scholarship for intelligent girls. Because you rescue black kittens. Also,' said Phryne, stopping and turning to face the girl, 'because I was very poor, as poor as I think you must have been, and I was rescued, and I think that I should return the favour. Does that answer your question?'

'Yes,' said Jane, much relieved, and followed Phryne into the house, where luncheon was on the table.

Chapter Six

*'I'm quite content to stay here—only I am
so hot and thirsty!'*
Alice Through the Looking Glass,
Lewis Carroll

Three o'clock was approaching, and the house was tense. The
only one who seemed unaffected by it was Jane, who spent the
afternoon consoling Ember after his bath, which he had not
enjoyed at all, and endeavouring to persuade him to accept the
collar as a mark of respect, instead of the instrument of feline
torture which was his first impression. She was not succeeding
very well, to judge by the number of times Phryne heard her
say, 'Now you have put all your paws into it again, you bad cat!'
There would be a pause while she disentangled the kitten, an
interlude while they played paperchase or had one of the light
meals which Mrs. Butler served to him, and then the litany
would begin again. When Phryne looked in at three, both Jane
and Ember had fallen asleep on Jane's bed. Phryne threw the
quilt over the two of them and closed the door.

Mrs. Butler was worrying about the milk, which might be on
the turn, and the dairy had not come today. Dot was worried
about the laundry, which had unaccountably lost three socks and

one of Phryne's cherished moss-green pillow cases. Phryne was tense on behalf of Miss Henderson, and Eunice, having surveyed her damaged face in a mirror for the first time, had burst into tears and taken to her bed, refusing to come out from under the covers until Dr. MacMillan had threatened that she should not see her young man at all.

This was enough to drag Eunice out from under the sheets, and when she had been anointed and dressed and veiled, she really was stunning. Phryne hoped that this young man was worth all this trouble, while reflecting cynically that no young man ever was.

The doorbell rang. Mr. Butler announced, 'Mr. Thompson and Mr. Herbert'. Aha! Perhaps the young man was as nervous about this visit as Eunice had been. If so, it showed a nice spirit. It would be up to her to entertain the friend, and Phryne sighed. She had sometimes questioned the ways of the All Wise Providence in His construction of young men. She would, however, entertain the companion, however taciturn or even spotty, with as good a grace as she could muster. After all, this was a murder inquiry, and she had deliberately chosen this profession. 'I could have stayed in Father's house and arranged flowers for the county,' she reminded herself, and swept forward to greet the visitors.

To her surprise and delight, they were very good looking. Both young men of medium height, with blond hair in an Eton crop, blue eyes, the fashionable flannel bags and the anyone-for-tennis blazer, the loose white 'artistic' shirts and the innovative wrist watches. Phryne had not seen one of these before. Both of them were as athletic and as sleek as otters. The lithe lines of the shoulder and hip spoke of smooth muscle and hidden power; these were not rowdies, but they were sportsmen of some sort.

They were dressed rather casually for a visit to a lady's house and the first young man eagerly explained.

'Miss Fisher? An honour to meet such a famous Sherlock. I'm Lindsay Herbert and this is Alastair Thompson. We apologize for our attire but we were training and the coach just wouldn't let us off, even though we explained about Miss Henderson.'

'Quite all right, gentlemen—do come in. Training for what?' asked Phryne casually, leading the way into her parlour and indicating seats before the fire. Lindsay sat down, but Alastair hovered.

'Dot, could you take Mr. Thompson to Miss Henderson, please? Just a moment, Mr. Thompson. Miss Henderson has gone through a terrible experience. You must be gentle with her and not ask her a lot of questions. She can't talk easily because of the burns, but she will not be scarred. Do you understand?' The young man drew himself up haughtily.

'I am a medical student, Miss Fisher, and I know how to talk to the sick. You have no need to be concerned.'

He followed Dot, and Lindsay laid a hand on Phryne's arm.

'Don't be angry, Miss Fisher, he doesn't mean to be so rude. He's been worried sick about Miss Henderson.'

'Yes, a terrible thing,' agreed Phryne. The hand on her arm was long and strong, and warm, even though it was sleeting again outside. She smiled at Lindsay, and patted the hand.

'Will she really be all right? And is she badly hurt?'

'The burns are not too bad, but the doctor is afraid of damage to the liver. Are you a medical student, too?'

'Lord, no, I'm a humble lawyer. Got to pass this year, you know, or the Pater will cut off supplies. I've been up at the Shop for five years, and this is the sixth.'

'Oh?' asked Phryne, scanning the perfect muscular curve of shoulder and throat. The firelight became him.

'Yes, I just could not get the hang of Contracts, and then I had to repeat Trusts, because I couldn't get the hang of them, either. In any case I'll be articled next year, and I'm most interested in crime. I shall go to the bar when the Pater can be convinced to stump up, and I shall specialize in crime. Fascinating. That's why I asked old Alastair to bring me along. I wanted to meet you.'

'Well, now you have met me,' said Phryne, leaning back in the leather armchair, 'what do you think?'

'Well, Miss Fisher, I'd heard you were good at puzzles, and I'd got it into my head that you were an old maid with a bent for detection—I never thought that you...that you...'

'That I?'

'Would be beautiful,' concluded Lindsay simply, and kissed the hand which lay along the top of the settee.

'Thank you. I'm glad that you came even when you thought I was an old maid. That shows dedication. What do you think of our little murder, then?'

'She was a really nasty old woman,' said the young man slowly. 'But it is a terrible thing to kill someone. A human, I mean, however horrible or superfluous, a breathing creature; a terrible responsibility, to take someone's death on yourself.'

'But that's what most murderers are like,' said Phryne. 'They are always sure that they are right, and that gives them the moral force to take on that burden. Or sometimes it is simpler; this person is in my way, and therefore they must die; because they are in my way, they do not deserve to live. I've heard that tune often enough.'

The young man appeared disconcerted at the vehemence of Phryne's discourse, and she changed the subject. One did not wantonly disconcert young men on whom one might be having designs in future.

And she might well have designs. A very pretty young man indeed, and predisposed by his odd interest in crime to be receptive.

'Training, you said?' Phryne poured the young man a drink—a weak brandy-and-water, at his request—and he took the glass and waved it enthusiastically.

'Rowing, Miss Fisher—on the river.'

Phryne suppressed the retort that she didn't think that it was on the land.

'I'm in the eight which might make the University team, Miss Fisher, but we have to keep up to the mark, so we are training all through the winter. You might like to come down and watch us. Our coach is a tartar, old Ellis.'

'Where do you train?' asked Phryne.

'Melbourne University boathouse, Miss, I can show you where it is, and we have some fine parties there, too.'

'Indeed?' Phryne was not concentrating. She was worried about Eunice, and caught herself agreeing to come and watch him training on the morrow before she realized what she had done. I really must start listening to what I am saying, she told herself firmly, but by then it was too late.

'Have you known Mr. Thompson long?'

'Lord, yes, we were at school together—Melbourne Grammar. I was quite a new chum then, coming from London, and the other fellows would have ragged me to death had it not been for Alastair. He's a good chap. I owe him a great deal,' said the young man solemnly. 'And he's very clever. A real shark at school for all those mathematics—I couldn't get the hang of them, either—and now they say he might win the surgery prize this year. He'll be a good doctor—sort of trustworthy, you know. But a nasty temper when aroused. We were playing football once, just a friendly game, and one of the forwards copped him one on the nose, and he gave a roar and pounced, and it took three men to pull him off the bully. But the nicest, kindest fellow you could meet,' he said hastily, 'a very good friend to me. I reckon there's nothing he couldn't do if he set his mind to it.'

Phryne replenished the brandy-and-water and asked her guest to show her his wrist watch. He exhibited it wrist and all, forcing Phryne to take his hand.

'It's a good watch, the Pater sent to New York for it—they are all the rage there, I'm told—and it keeps good time.' The hand and arm were now lying across Phryne's breasts, and her breathing jogged her nipples. 'I just have to be careful to keep it…out of…the water…'

His face was close, the mouth opening on a soft lip, his skin smelling of yellow soap and masculine sweat. Phryne abandoned herself and the arms circled her, the mouth closing on hers with emphasis and skill.

Phryne had retained her deep devotion to the male sex. She took care of her body, and her virtue took care of itself. The young man was sleek and strong, an intriguing combination, and had the promise of being a very fair lover indeed. But she did not have the time to indulge in spur-of-the-moment indiscretions on couches, and she detached herself gently, putting aside the hot mouth that kissed and clung.

'No, no, not now. Come back some time, my pretty young man, and I shall be delighted to receive you—but I'm too old to be seduced in front of a fire at four in the afternoon. Oh, you are lovely.' She kissed him again, just below the ear, where his hair curled enchantingly. 'Quite lovely.'

'Oh, Miss Fisher,' gasped Lindsay, dropping to his knees in front of her and burying his head in her shoulder, 'I think I've fallen in love with you!'

'Quite possibly,' agreed Phryne briskly. 'But it will wear off. I will come and watch you train tomorrow, as I promised when I wasn't myself, and then we may make some arrangements. But I am not toying with your heart, Lindsay—just your body. It is useless to fall in love with me—I do not want to damage you. Do you understand?'

'No,' confessed Lindsay, rubbing his face against her neck. 'But whatever you say, Miss Fisher.'

'I think,' conceded Phryne, 'that you had better call me Phryne.'

Mr. Herbert gulped his drink.

◇◇◇

Eunice Henderson, safe behind her veil, surveyed her lover with doting eyes. He was not tall, just the right size, and had delightful blue eyes, which were at present clouded with worry. He was worried about *her*! The thought was intoxicating. He, in turn, was struck with how elegant his fiancée looked. The green gown revealed the long, swooping line from hip to knee, the small waist, and the light curve of her small breasts. He sat down on the chair next to her bed and took her hand. It was hot, and he wondered what her temperature was.

'How do you feel, Eunice? I'm horrified by all this.'

'I feel much better. Miss Fisher has been very kind to me. She is also going to find out who killed Mother.'

'Oh. What about the burns, Eunice? I didn't know that chloroform would burn skin like that. Poor girl! What does the doctor say?'

'She says that it will heal without a scar if I don't scratch, though that is very hard, for it itches like fury. However, it doesn't hurt any more, and it really was painful. Ally, I thought I'd never bear the train journey to Melbourne. I only managed it because I was reading *Manon* and I could hide my face. I've got some ointment and the doctor says I should stay in bed for a week yet. I do feel weak. Were you worried about me?'

'My dear girl, can you doubt it? I was just about to storm Police Headquarters when the girl rang and told me where you were.'

He kissed the hand he was holding.

'Lindsay has gone to talk to Miss Fisher, he wanted to meet her, he's a crime buff. I bet he wouldn't like murder so much if he ever saw a corpse. What happened on that train, Eu? I've only read the press reports, and they are very highly coloured.'

'I don't know. I didn't wake until it was all over. Someone drugged the train, and dragged mother out of the window, no one knows how, and then she was found dead quite thirty feet from the track, and no one knows how she got there, either. It's all a terrible mystery. If it hadn't been for Miss Fisher the children on the train would have been dead, and the doctor still doesn't know if I'll have permanent liver damage. Can we talk about something else?'

'Oh, Eu, I had no idea that it was so bad! What would you like to talk about?'

'Us,' whispered Eunice. 'Now we can marry.'

'Of course we can, as soon as you are better. Let's put the notice in the paper tomorrow. The engagement is announced between Alastair, only son of William and Charlotte Thompson, of Right Street, Kew, and Eunice, only child of the late Walter and...' He faltered, and Eunice finished the notice:

'The late Anne Henderson of South Yarra. We can't put that in the paper, can we, with Mother not even buried? After the funeral, when I am up and about again, then we can marry. Unless you've changed your mind?'

'Oh, Eunice!' exclaimed Alastair Thompson, and embraced her with sufficient fervour to convince even the most obdurate lady that her swain had not changed his mind.

◇◇◇

Phryne, who was not obdurate, was swapping kisses and confidences with the second pretty young man in her house. Lindsay was ardent; his breath scorched her face; his lips were demanding and could prove engrossing; but Phryne's mind, which was seldom involved with her body at all, was ticking over nicely, and she was extracting much interesting information from Lindsay in between embraces.

'So you live in the same house as Alastair? What a comfortable arrangement. Who does the housekeeping?'

'Oh, a woman comes in every morning to make the beds and cook us some dinner to re-heat,' said Lindsay, insinuating a supple hand down Phryne's back. 'What involved undergarments you wear!'

'I shall teach you how to remove them,' promised Phryne. 'You will find that skill useful in years to come. But not now. Have you no sense of timing?'

'That's what the coach always says,' chuckled Lindsay, removing his hand. 'Very well, Miss Fisher, let us be proper. Alastair hasn't got much cash, see, his people are poor—respectable, I mean, his father's a doctor—but not much lettuce, so he lives with me. Pater gave me the house, and he pays for the housekeeper, and I like the company, so it all works out well. Amazing fellow, Alastair. I'm uncommonly fond of him. You know, even when he's strapped, he's never bitten me for a fiver till Thursday? None of the rest of my acquaintance have showed that restraint. Some of them look on me as a money tree…I like this fabric, it's so smooth. What is it?'

'Silk,' said Phryne, pulling down her skirt so that it almost reached her knees. 'It is supposed to be smooth and I'm glad that you like it. I think that it's about time that I flung you and your friend into the snow, Lindsay. I'll see you tomorrow. What time?'

'Nine in the morning,' said Lindsay, reluctantly releasing Phryne. 'At the boathouse. Why are you throwing us out? Have I lost my charm, already?'

'No, my dear, you have all the charm you came with. But I have to go and read a *post mortem* report, and talk to a policeman.'

'Can I come too?'

'No. I'll see you tomorrow.' She rang the bell. 'Mr. Butler, will you see the gentlemen out? And bring the car around. I've got to go into Russell Street.'

Lindsay collected his friend and left, not without a backward glance.

'Well, what did you think of them?' she asked Dot.

Dot grinned. 'Lindsay is all right, Miss, if you like Tom cats.'

'You know that I do,' agreed Phryne.

Chapter Seven

'You'll be catching a crab directly,' said Alice.
Alice Through the Looking Glass,
Lewis Carroll

Phryne steered the red car into the city. Detective-inspector Robinson (call me Jack, Miss Fisher, everyone does) had taken over the investigation and was anxious to interview her. He had promised the *post mortem* report and any more information that came to hand.

She parked her car in the police garage and ascended the dank stairs to the small bleak office which Jack inhabited. He looked up as she entered; an undistinguished youngish man with mid-brown hair and mid-brown eyes and no feature which one could remember more than three minutes after he had gone. It was this anonymity which had made him a relentless shadow of some of Melbourne's most wary crooks. They were now languishing behind bars, wondering how they had been detected, still not recalling the ordinary man on the street corner who had followed them doggedly for days. In private life he was a quiet man with a doting family who grew grevilleas and rare native orchids in his yard. He would talk learnedly of mulch unless instantly and firmly dissuaded.

'Ah, Miss Fisher. I hope that you are well? How nice to see you again. I won't offer you police-station tea, because I'm sure you've tasted it before. I want you to tell me all about the murder on the Ballarat train.'

'Delighted,' said Phryne promptly.

As usual, she told her tale with dispatch and not an unnecessary word. Detective-inspector Robinson took notes attentively.

'Dragged through the window, eh?'

'Absolutely. I'm almost sure that she was pulled up, because of the hair caught in the crack in the sill, but where the murderer was, I cannot tell.'

'And the blond young guard. Describe him.'

'About five-ten, blue eyes, a pleasant smile, looked well built but slender, no distinguishing marks except a scar on his fore-head. A cut along the brow line. All healed over. I think he was about twenty-five but he could have been younger, the cap is very disguising. I didn't pay much attention,' apologized Phryne. 'I was rather tired.'

'I could hope that all the witnesses that I interview weren't paying attention like that,' said the detective-inspector. 'What about motive?'

'The daughter had the best motive.' Phryne crossed her legs and tugged her black skirt down, lest she should distract the policeman. 'But I don't think that she did it. She could have shoved her mother out of the train and then doped herself. She might not have known that chloroform burns skin. I met her fiancé today, and he didn't know, and he's a medical student.'

'What did you make of him, Miss Fisher?'

'An arrogant young man, but most doctors are like that. About medium height, with pale hair and blue eyes, as was his pretty friend, they could be twins. Both strong, I should say, and active. It might be an idea to ask the attentive Mr. Thompson where he was on the night in question.'

'You didn't take to him, Miss Fisher?' asked the detective. 'What about the other one, his friend?'

'Lindsay Herbert. A very nice, if rather gushing and naïve, young man. I took to him, and he took to me, and stuck to me like glue, almost as if he had been instructed to do so.'

'What, Miss, did the young hound try to take advantage of you?' gasped the detective-inspector, and Phryne chuckled.

'If there is any advantage to be taken, Jack, you can rely on me to take it. I can cope with Master Lindsay. I didn't really have a chance to talk to Thompson. Perhaps you will have more success.'

'Perhaps. I shall certainly do so, and that at the earliest. Where do they live, these students?'

'In digs in Carlton, I fancy. But I know where they will be at nine tomorrow morning.'

'Where?'

'Rowing. I am going down to the boathouse to watch them practice. Perhaps you would like to come too?'

'Yes, Miss Fisher, I think that I might.'

'Good. Now, the autopsy report.'

Phryne scanned the buff folder critically, attempting to translate the medical terms into something that might relate to the broken body of the old woman. It seemed that all of the gross fractures had been inflicted after death, including the massive blow which had cracked the skull. The cause of death had been…

'Hanging? That's what that means, isn't it, Jack? Fracture of the cervical vertebrae?'

'Yes, Miss. Hanging it is. The hyoid bone in the throat which is always broken when there is a death by strangulation was fractured but the doctor says that it was a broken neck. That's how you die if you are hanged, Miss. The sudden jerk.' He mimed the rope pulling taut and the sickening flop of the broken neck, and Phryne shuddered.

'Don't, Jack, please, it's too awful. What could have happened? The first bit is clear. Someone doped the carriage and sent us all to sleep, and perhaps we were meant to sleep forever. Then no one would be able to tell when the body was removed, or how, but I woke up too soon. How that murderer must be disliking me, for I foiled his little plan proper. All right, the carriage is full of people all asleep, and the old woman is dragged out—with a rope around her neck?—suspended, and dropped.'

'Don't forget the Ballan doctor's theory.'

'The man is deranged, it's too ghastly to contemplate.'

'And how is the girl, the one who lost her memory?'

'Jane? I call her Jane, she hasn't remembered. I shall have a photographer take some pictures of her, and perhaps you can have them distributed among the stations and your staff. Someone must have lost her. I'm keeping her anyway, she's been molested, and if that is what triggered her off, then I am going to skin the man alive if she remembers who he is. She's a very clever girl and I expect to have her recalling her past any day now.'

'Sexually molested?'

'So Dr. MacMillan says.'

'Poor little thing. You'll let me in on the arrest, Miss Fisher, as usual?'

'You will have to be quick,' said Phryne grimly, and Jack Robinson nodded.

'You didn't kill that child-molesting bastard we arrested in Queenscliff,' he said gently. 'Even though you did shoot him a bit.'

'That's because I promised to deliver him to you in a plain brown wrapper,' said Phryne reasonably. 'This one is all mine.'

Wisely, the detective-inspector decided not to pursue the subject, and returned to the matter of murder on the Ballarat train.

'I've checked up on all the guards and railway employees on that train, by the way, and Wallace was right—not one of them under forty. You are sure that it was a young man?'

'Positive,' said Phryne, recalling the smooth, unlined throat and chin.

'I shall see you tomorrow, then, Miss Fisher—at the Melbourne University boathouse,' and the policeman escorted Phryne out of the building and down the steps. She was restless, aroused by the ardent young man's attentions, and decided to pass some blameless hours in the museum and art gallery. There she spent some time before the Apollo, a copy of the Belvedere, and tore her salacious mind away with some difficulty.

Phryne was home in time for a pleasant dinner and a bath, then put herself to bed early, sober and alone.

◇◇◇

Dot woke Phryne with a cup of Turkish coffee at eight-thirty, and informed her half-asleep mistress that it was a nasty damp chill morning, but that it was not actually raining. She added that Mr. Butler had taken Jane to the photographer and that Miss Henderson was still asleep. Phryne absorbed the coffee, which was as close as one got to neat caffeine, washed, and dressed in boots, trousers, and a heavy jacket. Dot found a suitable hat and an umbrella and gloves and assisted Phryne to start the huge car.

'I must have been mad to agree with this,' she commented. 'Steady she goes, Dot. Thanks, go inside quickly before you freeze to the spot. Back directly,' she called, and put the Hispano-Suiza into gear.

She drove without haste, threading the traffic through the city and out onto the road which circled the gardens, finding the turn without backing more than enough to ruin the temper. The track down to the boathouse was rough, but not too muddy, and the big car negotiated it with ease. She stopped and got out, and the first thing that she saw was a long wooden shell with eight pairs of legs, locomoting down to the water.

A further glance showed her that this was a racing boat being carried by its crew. She waved, and a forest of hands waved back; evidently the crew were not used to being watched while training, and appreciated the company. A small man, thin, with a red face and fanatic's eyes, was climbing onto a very new and shiny bicycle.

He gave Phryne a disapproving glare in passing, and wobbled down onto the towing path. The crew had dropped their boat neatly into the water, where it seemed to float as light as a leaf, and then they all hopped in with scarcely a ripple, oars extended. Phryne saw the beautiful Lindsay and Alastair, who was rowing stroke. He still looked nervous and strained. Phryne heard the command: 'Racing start! Three quarter!' and the boat slid quickly into the stream. 'Half!' and the oars feathered and dipped with speed. 'Three quarter and go!' and the boat was moving swiftly down the waterway, the coach toiling alongside on his bicycle. They were under the bridge, and Phryne had to strain her eyes to see them. By one of those freaks caused by the combination of sound and water, she heard the command 'Bow and two!' and the boat spun on its axis and sped down the river towards her. It seemed to be travelling quite fast, and the coach was toiling over his handlebars. This did not interrupt his breath in the slightest, and he was shouting opprobrious epithets like a sergeant-major.

'Jones, pull your stomach in! Get your hands round that oar, Hoskins! You aren't stirring soup! What's the matter with you, Herbert, dreaming about your lady friend? Put your back into it! Catch! Finish! Catch! Finish!'

He roared to a halt and glared as the crew regained the boathouse.

'You row like a lot of schoolgirls! How do you row?'

'Like schoolgirls, sir,' came the obedient chorus, and Mr. Ellis grunted, seeming to breathe fire through his nostrils. 'That's right! That so-called racing start was slower than a nurse and a pram! So we do it again! And if you are still thinking about your lady friends,' here he gave Phryne a furious look, whiffling the ends of his bristly black moustache, 'or your breakfasts, you'll never make the team! All right! Racing start! And this time, keep your minds on what you are doing!'

The crew lifted the oars again, and Phryne wandered away from the bank and found a seat and lit a cigarette. She had a book in her pocket and was just wondering whether Lindsay would be mortally offended if she read it, when she glanced up and saw the sight of the year, which more people claimed to have witnessed than would have fitted on the bank, even standing on each other's shoulders.

The choleric coach, aroused to apoplexy by some fault in the crew's performance, raised his megaphone to curse them heartily and found that there was a dip in the towing path. With a final, full-throated cry of 'schoolgirls!' he careered down the bank, losing control of the bike but retaining his grip on the megaphone, and with a muffled 'Argh!' was seated on the bicycle and clutching the megaphone in seven feet of water. The boat swept past, full of rowers so paralysed with shock that they did not know how to react, and so appalled that they did not dare to laugh. They turned at the bridge and came back, extending an oar for Ellis to hang on to, but he had struggled to the shore by then and was standing by the boathouse, muddy and dripping, dredging river weed from his megaphone.

'Be here tomorrow, and be on time,' was all he said, and stalked away, while Phryne bit her finger to still the hysteria which threatened to choke her. The crew carried the shell out of the water and stowed it and the oars, by which time the coach had disappeared around the corner. Lindsay howled with mirth, followed by all but the serious Alastair.

'Oh, oh, my ribs will crack!' protested Lindsay, hanging on to Phryne's shoulder as she wiped her eyes. 'He'll never live it down, never. Poor old Ellis! Schoolgirls! Well, Miss Fisher, you can't say that we aren't amusing company. I'll just have a shower and change, and then I'll be at your service. If you don't mind waiting?'

Phryne inclined her head, and was instantly the centre of a vocal group. It appeared that her reputation as a detective had gone before her.

'Would you come along and talk to some of the fellows, Miss Fisher?' asked an eager young man. 'We'd love to hear about your experiences.'

I bet you would, thought Phryne. But you aren't going to.

'I am talking to the fellows,' she temporized, 'and you should get an introduction to a real detective. I'm just an amateur. Are you all students?'

'Yes, Miss Fisher, but in different faculties. Edwards and Johnson are Music, Herbert and Tommy Jones are Commerce, Thompson and Connors are Medicine and the other Herbert is

Law. I'm Arts, unlike all these blundering oafs. Just now we are pondering whether it would be better to request the ladies to join us in song and beer, but mostly song, as our glee club is running out of glees which sound good with only tenor and bass.'

'The trouble with scoring the Elizabethan stuff for the male voice is that it all sounds so Russian,' complained one of the music students. 'And a little of that goes a long way, you know.'

'I agree entirely. What's wrong with asking the ladies to join?'

'Well, it seems silly, but we are all friends together, and we get drunk together and no one minds, and we tend to sing rather rude songs, and the ladies…'

'Shall we make a little bet?' suggested Phryne. 'Put your groups together for some madrigals, and I'll bet you five pounds to a row down the river in a real boat that they know much ruder ones.'

'Bet,' said the Arts student instantly. 'My name is Black, Miss Fisher, Aaron Black, and I'm by way of being convenor of the Glee Club. We'll ask the girls, because we want to do the Brahms *Liebeslieder*, and we shall have a bit of a sing in the boathouse on—say, Friday? Yes? And will you come, too? I know that the ladies would love to meet you—and I'm sure that you can sing. Unlike Tommy over there, who is tone deaf.'

'Yes, I can sing,' agreed Phryne. 'What time? And shall I bring anything?'

'Some beer would be nice,' said Aaron Black. 'You will come, then?'

'If that place has any heating, yes.'

'It shall be heated, if I have to bribe the furnace man with gold,' said Aaron. 'Till then, Miss Fisher.'

Alastair passed her on his way into the boathouse, but he did not say a word. Phryne went back thoughtfully to sit in the car and was presently joined by Lindsay, clean and dressed in old flannels and a cricket jumper.

'I never thought that you'd really come,' he said quietly. 'I am honoured, Miss Fisher.'

'Get in,' invited Phryne, 'I'm freezing here. What nice fellows your crewmates are. They've invited me to a sing-song in the boathouse on Friday. Are you coming? Can you sing?'

'Yes, and yes,' agreed the young man, slicking back his hair. 'Nothing would keep me away from you, Phryne. And I carol a very neat stave, if I do say so myself.'

'Sing to me,' requested Phryne. 'Shall you come home with me?' she added, with such hidden emphasis that Lindsay's admirable jaw dropped.

'Yes,' he stammered, and Phryne started the car.

As they negotiated the muddy path, the young man began to sing, in a pure, unaccented tenor:

Since making whoopee became all the rage,
It's even got into the old bird cage,
My canary has circles under his eyes...

Chapter Eight

'I never put things into people's hands—that would never do—you must get it for yourself.'
Alice Through the Looking Glass,
Lewis Carroll

'I should like a word with you, if you please,' said an undistinguished man courteously, flashing a badge. Alastair was leaving the boathouse in search of any vehicle which was going to Carlton when a hand fell on his shoulder. 'I'm Detective-inspector Robinson, and I'm investigating the murder of Mrs. Henderson. I gather that you know her daughter.'

'Yes, I do, we are engaged to be married. I don't know anything about the murder.'

'Just for the record, sir, where were you on the night of the twenty-first of June?' asked the policeman, taking out a notebook. 'Perhaps we might sit down on this seat here, you look tired.'

'I'm not tired,' snapped the young man. 'And I'm not telling you anything. I don't have to tell you what I was doing.'

'No, sir, you don't have to tell me, but if you don't then I will have to find out, and it would be easier all round if you told me,' said the detective easily. 'That was the night of the murder, and I will be asking all of the persons involved what they were doing. Just for elimination, you understand. Were you at home?'

'I suppose so,' agreed Alastair grudgingly. Detective-inspector Robinson made a laborious note.

'I see, and was anyone with you?'

'No. My room-mate was out. All night. I don't know where he was, either. You'll have to ask him.'

'I don't see what business it is of mine, as he isn't involved with this matter at all.'

'Oh, isn't he? I tell you one thing, that female harpy has got her claws into him. She collected him like a parcel and he's gone off with her in her big red car.'

'Well, that's not my affair either, is it? Or yours, sir.' Robinson did not correct the young man, although he knew that harpies are always female. Robinson had been to a public school.

'That's none of my concern. What were you doing, at home and all alone? Did anyone call?'

'No. I was quite alone all night and I can't prove it. So put that in your pipe and smoke it,' added the young man fiercely. 'I don't have to answer to you! And unless you want to arrest me now, I'm going home.'

'I'm not arresting you,' said the policeman calmly, 'yet.'

'Then I'm going,' said Alastair defiantly. He walked a few paces, stopped and glared, as if defying Robinson to make a move, then strode away.

'Well, that may be the product of injured innocence, and it may not,' mused the detective-inspector. 'A little more inquiry should settle it. And Miss Fisher has taken the other one home with her, has she?' he chuckled. 'Pity I can't use her methods of interrogation. I'm sure that they would be more fun.' He went back to his police car and drove decorously back to Russell Street.

On arrival, he found a packet of photographs on the desk, with a note from Dot.

'Dear Mr. Robinson,' he read. Dot still did not like policemen, but she did like Robinson, so she did not use his title. 'Miss Fisher said to send these to you. She also wants me to tell you that the girl is five feet tall, weighs six stone, and has brown eyes and brown hair. She has no distinguishing—' Dot had taken several tries to manage this word—'marks or scars except a brown mole on her right upper arm. She says that she has had the pictures taken in the old frock she wore on the train, and hopes that you can find out who lost her. Yours truly, Dorothy Williams (Miss).'

The photographs showed a thin, pale young woman with long hair. Anyone who knew the girl ought to recognize her from them. The detective-inspector called up his minions, sent out the negative plates to be copied and distributed, and also ordered a discreet watch on the angry medical student. 'Just,' he said to himself, 'in case.'

◇◇◇

Phryne arrived home, found that Dot and Jane had gone back with Dr. MacMillan to the Queen Victoria Hospital to observe casualty, and Miss Henderson was ensconced for the day in her bed with a new novel. Mrs. Butler was expecting the dairy-boy and the baker, and so was relieved of her anxieties in the matter of the milk. Phryne put in an order for hot chocolate and raisin toast and led the bemused young man up the stairs to her private chambers.

These were decorated in her favourite shade of green; curtains and carpets were mossy, and even the sheets on her bed were leaf-coloured. It was a little like being in a tree, the young man thought, as he sank down onto a couch which yielded luxuriously to his weight and seemed to embrace his limbs.

Lindsay Herbert had seen many movies, and he was reminded forcibly of Theda Bara in *Desire*. She, however, had reclined on a tigerskin rug, and Miss Fisher had only common sheepskin.

The fire was lit, the room was warm, and Lindsay was alert, aroused, and tense. Had she brought him here only to tease him, to raise him to an unbearable pitch of desire and then to disappoint him? He had known such women. He hoped that Phryne was not one of them, but he was neither sure nor certain, and sipped his hot chocolate suspiciously.

He began to realize that she was in earnest when she dismissed Mr. Butler, told him that she was not to be disturbed, and threw the bolt on the door. Now these three rooms were cut off from the rest of the house, although household noises could be heard through the floor; the voice of Mrs. Butler giving the dairy-man a piece of her mind in reference to the soured milk of yesterday, and the noise of Mr. Butler using the new vacuum cleaner on the hall carpet.

Lindsay put down the cup and stood up, and Phryne put a record on the gramophone. She wound it up with some force and placed the needle on the spinning disc, and there was Bessie Smith, the thin, feline voice, lamenting, 'He's a woodpecker, and I just knock on wood…'

Phryne slid into Lindsay's arms and whispered, 'Let's dance.' They began to foxtrot slowly to the woman's lament. Lindsay was keenly alive to the scent of Miss Fisher's hair, the smoothness of her bare arms, and when she raised her head, he laid his mouth to her throat and clutched her close.

'Oh, Phryne,' he breathed and her voice came, cool and amused.

'Do you want me?'

'You know I do.'

'Well, I want you, too,' she returned, her hands dropping to the buttons of his shirt. The song ground to an end and the gramophone ran down. Phryne peeled off the young man's shirt and caressed the shoulders and back, smooth and lithe and muscular, unblemished, young. Here were no hard lumps of football muscle, but the long sinews of a runner. Lindsay, striving to control hands that trembled, undid the hook at the back of Miss Fisher's beautiful woollen dress, and then fumbled his way down until the dress dropped, and she was revealed in bust-band and petticoat and gartered stockings. He noticed that she had jazz garters, all colours, as she sat down on the couch and extended her legs for him to remove them. As he rolled the silk, trying not to snag it, he relished the smoothness of her naked skin, and saw that she, too, trembled at his touch.

The petticoat, it appeared, came off over her head, and the bust-band undid at the back.

Phryne took her lover by the hand and led him to her big bed, in the warm room, and lay down. Her body seemed almost luminous against the dark-green sheets, and Lindsay, for a moment, was overcome and thought that he might faint. Her scent was musky now, female and demanding, and he was afraid that he might hurt her.

She wriggled a little, and was underneath him; he was not sure how she had got there. He felt the delicate bones, overlaid with fine skin, at her hip and her chest; ran his hands down her sides as she thrust up her breasts to his mouth.

As the lips closed, Phryne gave a soft cry, and Lindsay was inside her, the strong but liquid, blood-heat tissue and muscle clutching and sucking, and Lindsay realized that she did not mean to cheat him.

All previous half-frightened, half-bold encounters in bushes, which had been the pitch of his sexual experience before, vanished before this bath of sensuality. The woman was strong and as lithe as a cat; she twisted and moved beneath and above him, stroking and kissing; she loved the touch of his hands and body in the same way as he loved the contact of her skin on his own. He detected the ripple of her desire as it reached its climax; he fell forward onto her body as she flexed and gasped and was clutched close in her arms.

Lindsay Herbert buried his face in Phryne's shoulder and began to weep.

Phryne, assuaged, held him close, his tears pooling in the hollow of her collarbone, until he sniffed and shook his head, and then she said gently, 'Are you regretting the loss of your innocence, my dear?'

The young man raised a glowing, wet face to hers and said, 'Oh, no, no, it was just so lovely, so lovely, Phryne, I couldn't bear it to end…I mean…'

Phryne released him and he rolled away to dry his eyes on the sheet. He laid a calloused hand on her thigh, and laughed. Phryne sat up.

'If that is the joy of conquest, my sweet darling, then I can't approve of it. Come and lie down again. I like the feel of your body, Lindsay—you are an intriguing mixture of smooth and strong.'

He stretched out beside her and yawned.

'I thought that you were a vamp,' he said artlessly, and was mildly offended when Phryne began to laugh. 'No, don't laugh at me. I mean, vamps always lead men on, and arouse them, and then abandon them.'

'Well, I certainly aimed to arouse lust,' agreed Phryne, gurgling with suppressed laughter, 'but I had no intention of leaving you unsatisfied. And there's no hurry, my sweet. We can stay here all day. Unless you have something else to do?'

Lindsay pulled a grim face.

'You realize that you've made me miss three lectures,' he reproved, and Phryne pulled him down into her arms again.

'And I shall make you miss another three,' she said, sealing his protesting mouth with her own. Lindsay knew when he had met a determined woman. He submitted.

◇◇◇

Miss Henderson, on inquiring as to the whereabouts of Miss Fisher, was told by Mr. Butler that she was in conference and could not be disturbed. Mr. Butler's face was perfectly straight. He was pleased that Miss Fisher had dropped the painter who had been her last lover. The painter had left partly-finished canvases all over the place and had washed his brushes in Mrs. Butler's pristine kitchen sink. A law student, Mr. Butler reflected, was likely to be much cleaner around the house.

◇◇◇

Awakening from a light sleep, Lindsay turned over with a muttered curse, loath to leave the most ravishing dream he had enjoyed for…well, for all of his life. His face came into contact with Phryne's sleeping breast and he woke, and kissed her.

'Oh, Phryne, so you weren't a dream!'

'Quite real and indeed palpable,' agreed Phryne. 'But I must get up, Lindsay darling. I've got things to do.'

'Yes, I know,' said the young man, holding her firmly and pinning her down with one knee. 'Later.'

'Later,' Phryne succumbed, laughing.

◇◇◇

Lindsay was in the bathroom, wondering which of the golden dolphin taps would yield hot water, when there was a thunderous banging at the front door, and he heard the admirable Mr. Butler open it.

'I must see Miss Henderson,' he heard Alastair say, in a muted roar which meant that he was very angry indeed. Phryne pulled on a robe and joined him in listening.

'Very well, sir, if you would care to wait I will ascertain if she is at home,' Mr. Butler replied.

Alastair yelled, 'You know she's at home!'

Mr. Butler said crushingly, 'I meant, sir, that I would find out if she is at home to you.'

There was a silence, during which they could hear feet pacing to and fro across the tiles of the landing. The door to Miss Henderson's room opened and shut.

'Miss Henderson will see you, sir.'

The feet ran down the hall. Phryne heard the door crash open.

'Eunice, have you had the infernal nerve to call in the police?' shouted Alastair, and Phryne swore.

'Hell! Has the man no heart? What did I do with my clothes?'

She dragged on some garments and ran down the stairs, with the half-naked Lindsay close behind her.

'Mr. Thompson, I must ask you not to make such a noise!' she said icily, and he turned on her a face white with fury.

'You traitorous bitch! What have you done with my friend? All you women are alike—all betrayers and whores!'

He swung back his arm, meaning to slap Phryne across the face, and found himself on his knees with a terrible pain in his elbow. Miss Fisher's face, calm and cold, was three inches from his own, and he could smell the scent of female sexuality exuding from her skin. It turned him sick.

'Make one move and I'll break your arm,' said Miss Fisher flatly. 'What do you mean, storming into my house like a bully? Call me a traitor, will you? Here is your friend. I haven't hurt him. I have pleased him—and perhaps that's more than you could have done, hmm? Go on. Try to hit me again.'

Lindsay, aghast, had stopped on the stairs when he realized that Phryne did not need any help. The fight was going out of Alastair. At the same time, Dot and Jane came to the front door, Miss Henderson started to cry, Mr. Butler picked up the telephone to call the police and Mrs. Butler appeared from the kitchen with the poker. Alastair stood up slowly, glared at Phryne, turned, and walked out of the house.

'The fun's over,' said Phryne, pushing back her hair. 'Come down, Lindsay. Mr. B., shut the door, and serve some drinks. Don't distress yourself, Miss Henderson, it's just a brainstorm of some kind, he'll be better tomorrow. Dot, Jane, how nice to see you. Come in and I think I will open a bottle of champagne, Mr. B. It has been a very good day, otherwise.'

Phryne sank down on the couch and set about dispelling the sour aftertaste of Alastair's violence with vivacity and Veuve Clicquot.

Chapter Nine

'Although she managed to pick plenty of
beautiful Rushes…there was always a more
lovely one that she couldn't reach.'

Alice Through the Looking Glass,
Lewis Carroll

Phryne woke from an uncomfortable dream—not precisely a
nightmare but certainly not a delightful reverie—and found that
during the night she had pulled a pillow over her face, which
probably accounted for it.

Next to her, sleeping like a baby, lay the beautiful Lindsay, as
sleek as a seal, and utterly relaxed. Phryne picked up his hand,
and dropped it. It fell limply.

'Out to the world,' she observed, and went to the bathroom
to run herself a deep, hot, foaming bath, scented with 'Rose de
Gueldy'. Then she sat down on the big bed and looked at her
lover, finding herself unexpectedly moved by his beauty and
his gentleness. Her motives in seducing him had been mixed,
to say the least; among them lust and the desire to hammer a
wedge between him and his friend Alastair predominated. He
had been an engrossing, untiring, eager lover and an apt pupil,
and she almost envied the lucky young woman whom he would

marry. Like Janet in the old ballad of Tam Lin, 'she had gotten a stately groom'.

He sighed and turned over, revealing the ordered propriety of bone and muscle that was his back, and Phryne was about to slide down beside him again when she bethought herself of her bath, and went to take it, getting to the taps seconds before it overflowed.

She soaked herself thoroughly, and only rose from the foam like Aphrodite when Mr. Butler tapped at the door with the early morning tea.

'Good morning, Mr. Butler,' she said, accepting the loaded tray, and the houseman smiled at her.

'Good morning, Miss Fisher, you are looking well, the young man has done you good. I've brought the papers, Miss Jane's photograph is in them.'

'Thank you, Mr. Butler,' and Phryne shut the door, woke Lindsay with a cup of tea, and sat down beside him to survey the news.

Jane's photograph occupied a column of page three, with the caption, 'Do you know this girl?' Phryne thought that it had come out uncommonly well, and should produce results. Lindsay sat up sleepily and drank his tea, and Phryne settled back comfortably against his shoulder.

'I don't know if I dare go back to my digs,' confessed the young man who had done Miss Fisher so much good. 'How can I look old Alastair in the eye?'

'Mmm?' asked Phryne and Lindsay tried to explain.

'You see, we've known each other almost all our lives, and we've always done everything together—we used to climb together, but Alastair had an accident with another climber. He was killed by a falling rock, and Alastair thought that it was his fault, though it wasn't, of course, rocks can happen to anyone, then we were in the school play together—he was a good actor. I remember him doing Captain Hook, limping around waiting for the crocodile...tick...tick...with his face all scarred.'

'Oh? How did he do that?' asked Phryne, who was not really listening.

'Glue, Phryne—just glue. You must have noticed how it puckers up your skin if you spill it. A line of glue on the face and there's your scar. Perfect. Then we joined the Glee Club, and because we couldn't climb anymore, he suggested that we take up rowing, and we've always done everything together, except…'

'Except this,' said Phryne, kissing him on his swollen mouth. 'But it was bound to happen, Lindsay. Didn't you feel left out when he took up with Miss Henderson?'

'Well, no, she never seduced him, and I always thought her a very dull girl, with that frightful mother. I could never understand what he saw in her, really. A very good girl, of course, but no conversation. She used to just sit there and adore him and her mother would sit there and abuse him, and I refused to go there again, I just couldn't see the amusement in it. But he seemed devoted, though he never talked about her. Then again, words could not express what I feel about you, so there it is. And I must get up and go to training,' said the young man reluctantly. 'Shall I see you again?'

'Do you want to?'

'More than anything else.'

'Then you shall. But not tonight. I shall see you Friday at the Glee Club singalong, and you shall come home with me again, if you like. Today's Wednesday. That should give you time to recover.'

'I'll never recover,' declared Lindsay Herbert gallantly, and escorted Phryne down to breakfast.

Lindsay was just about to leave when the doorbell rang and Mr. Butler allowed a crestfallen Alastair to enter. The student was bearing a huge bundle of out-of-season roses and did not even start when he came face to face with Lindsay and Phryne.

'I came to say how sorry I was about that scene yesterday,' he said in a low voice, thrusting the flowers at Phryne. She sidestepped neatly.

'Take them to Miss Henderson, she's the one you have hurt.'
Phryne's voice was cold. 'You didn't do me any harm.'

'Lindsay, old man, I'm sorry,' said Alastair, and Lindsay took
his hand and shook it warmly.

'That's all right, Alastair. I'll wait for you and we shall go to
training together.'

Lindsay sat down in the hall and Alastair went to make peace
with his fiancée.

From the cry of delight which Phryne heard from outside the
door, where she was unashamedly listening, it seemed that he
had succeeded. He came out five minutes later, collected Lindsay,
and went off down the path, a picture of humility.

Dot wondered that Phryne shut the door behind them with
such a vindictive slap.

The phone rang as she was walking down the hall, and Phryne
took the call herself.

'Yes, this is Miss Fisher…yes, the Honourable Phryne Fisher,'
Dot heard Phryne say impatiently. 'A missing girl? Where was she
last seen?' She was scribbling notes on the telephone book. 'I see,
outside Emily MacPherson? Someone actually saw her go? Good.
A description of the abductor please…yes. Portly but respectable…all right. Do you have a photograph of her? Good. And
some idea of her destination? Oh, dear. I see. Gertrude Street, eh?
She has been seen there? By whom? Never mind, I suppose that I
don't need to know that, really. Send me the photograph and I'll
do what I can. Yes, Mr. Hart, I will reassure her that you still want
her…of course. Send the photograph as soon as you can. You shall
have her home soon if that is where she is. Goodbye.'

'What is it, Miss?'

'Troubles rarely come singly, Dot. That was a Mr. Hart
who wants me to retrieve his daughter Gabrielle from a brothel
in Fitzroy, whence she was enticed from outside the Emily
MacPherson School of Domestic Science by a portly but respectable gentleman. And her father wants her back, convinced that she
has been mesmerized. It sounds highly unlikely to me. However,
I shall take the photo and do the brothel rummage with Klara.

She knows everyone on Gertrude Street. Nothing I can do until the picture arrives. Now who is calling, for God's sake?'

It was the estate manager. Phryne stamped into her salon and awaited him with scant patience. She was not in the mood for business.

Phryne spent an irritating morning arguing with Mr. Turner who wanted her to buy more shares. Phryne was acquiring land, and selling off her speculative shares, sometimes even at a loss. The only ones she consented to keep were beer, tobacco, and flour.

'I don't care,' she finally shouted, out of all patience with the man. 'I don't care if shares in some Argentinian gold mine are going cheap. They can't be cheap enough for me. I want houses and I want government stocks, and that's all I want, except perhaps some more jewellery. That is my last word, and if you do not carry out my wishes, I will find a solicitor who can. Mr. Butler, see Mr. Turner out!'

Mr. Turner left, taking his hat more in sorrow than in anger, and Mr. Butler shut him out. Mr. Turner turned back on the porch, as though he had thought of yet another stock which Miss Fisher might find more acceptable, but Mr. Butler had locked the door. He was sorry that his mistress was in such a tiz, and put his head around the kitchen door to warn his wife that lunch had better be early and good, because Miss Fisher was going to need a drink.

Miss Fisher, however, did not get the chance. Another caller hung on the bell, and this time Mr. Butler was faced with a tall, raw-boned woman, who demanded, 'Where's my niece?'

Mr. Butler was about to tell her to drink beer next time, because gin obviously gave her the heeby jeebies, when she flourished a photograph torn out of a newspaper. It was Jane's photograph.

'Perhaps you should speak to Miss Fisher, then, Mrs....'

'Miss,' she snarled. 'Miss Gay.'

Mr. Butler went regretfully to Phryne to warn her that someone had come to remove Jane. Phryne came out into the hall with outstretched hand, at the same time as Jane emerged from her room, with Ember riding on her shoulder.

'There she is. My niece. I want her back!'

'Do you?' asked Phryne unpleasantly. 'I see. Jane, do you remember this...lady?'

Jane had shrunk back against the wall, frightened by the strident voice and the clutching hand.

'Of course she remembers me!' shrieked Miss Gay, who seemed to be singularly badly named. 'I'm her Aunt Jessie and she's my niece Jane Graham, and if you didn't know her name why did you call her Jane?'

'I plucked a name out of the air, and I don't think she recalls you, do you, Jane?'

Jane shook her head, numbly. Phryne turned Miss Gay by the sleeve.

'Leave me your address, and some proofs that she is your niece, and I'll have my lawyer look them over. I really can't release Jane into your custody until I am sure that she is your relative. And possibly not then. What were you about, to let her get that thin, and be on a train to Ballarat all on her own?'

'I pinned her ticket into her pocket, and she was lucky to get the job, going as a skivvy in a doctor's house, she was, though I suppose they've got someone else for the job now. Don't listen to her if she says that I mistreated her...I treated her like one of my own, so I did, when her mother died, and then her grand-mother died...'

'Yes, thank you, Miss Gay, what is your address?' asked Phryne, and wrote it down. 'I'll be in touch with you in due course, or my solicitor will. You are the girl's legal guardian, I assume? Appointed by a Court? No? I thought not. Good morning, Miss Gay.'

Phryne stepped back as she gave the woman a shrewd push and shoved her out of the house in mid-sentence.

'Quick, Mr. Butler, shut that door, bolt it and bar it, don't let anyone in. I am not at home to anyone, not even a long lost relative or a man telling me I have won Tatt's. Gosh, what a morning! Jane? Where are you?'

Jane was crushed into the corner of her bed, with an indignant Ember in her arms, and Phryne did not touch her. She sat down on the end of the bed and said casually, 'I'm not going to give you up, you know. That woman has no claim on you. Even if you are Jane Graham, and it's a nice name, I like it, she can't make you live with her. She isn't your guardian and she may not be your closest relative. So don't worry. I'll call my solicitor and have him draw up adoption papers at once. In fact, I'll call him now. Have you remembered anything?'

'Sort of. I began to remember when Ember scratched on the window. My name is Jane Graham. I recall my grandmother but I don't remember that woman at all. As far as I know, I've never seen her before. What's the address, Miss Fisher?'

'Seventeen Railway Crescent, Seddon.'

Jane shook her head again.

'No.'

'Not a bell?'

'No.'

'You can tell me the truth, you know. I've given you my word that you shall stay with me, and I am not forsworn.'

'Miss Fisher, I am telling you the truth. I don't recall the address and I don't know the name. I can remember everything up to my grandmother's death. Then it's all a fog.'

'What was in the parcel we took with us on the train?'

'Rachel coloured rice powder and Lalla perfume, a collar for Ember and some flea-soap, and…and…there was something else…the chrysanthemums for Dot. I think that's all.'

'There's nothing wrong with your memory, is there, Jane?'

Jane shook her head, so that the heavy plaits danced.

'No. I can remember everything that happened from the time I was on Ballarat station, but nothing of the past until my grandmother's funeral.'

'I know who we need,' said Phryne briskly. 'We need Bert and Cec. I'll go and call them now.'

'Bert?' asked Jane, bewildered but uncoiling from her defensive crouch.

'And Cec,' agreed Phryne, on her way to the phone. She dialled, and asked the operator for an address in Fitzroy.

'Bert? It's Phryne Fisher. I've got a bit of a job for you. Are you on?'

The telephone quacked, seeming to expostulate.

'No, no, nothing rough, or illegal, just a spot of investigating. Excellent. See you in an hour,' and Phryne rang off. She smiled at Jane.

'There's just time for lunch, and then we shall send out the troops. Don't look so downcast, pet. You are staying with me, come Hell or high water. If you remember anything else, anything at all, tell me. Now—lunch.'

Because of Mr. Butler's warning and because of her own culinary pride, Mrs. Butler served up a *riz de veau financiére* of superlative tenderness and flavour, followed by a selection of cheeses and a compôte of winter fruits. Phryne had two glasses of a nice dry Barossa, which she was trying for a vintner friend, and was in an expansive mood when Bert and Cec arrived in their shiny new taxi.

They came in and sat down, uneasy in Phryne's delicate salon, and were introduced.

'This is Jane Graham, or at least, we think she is. Have you seen the papers today?'

Bert nodded. Cec grunted.

'Jane, this is Mr. Albert Johnson, a staunch friend of mine.' Jane looked at Bert. He was short and stocky, with shrewd blue eyes and a thatch of dark hair, thinning at the crown. He was wearing a threadbare blue suit and a clean white shirt, evidently newly donned. He smiled at Jane.

'And this is Mr. Cecil Yates, Bert's mate; you should get on, he loves cats.'

Ember gave a mute vote of confidence by leaping up onto Cec's knee and climbing his coat. Cec stroked him gently. He was tall and Scandinavian looking, with a mane of blond hair and incongruous deep brown eyes like a spaniel. He nodded at Jane.

Bert gave the kitten a polite pat and said, 'Well, Miss, what's the go?'

'Jane was given to me to mind, because she was found on the Ballarat train in a skimpy little dress I wouldn't have clothed a dog in, with a second-class ticket in her pocket and no memory of who she was or how she got there. Today a frightful woman arrived and demanded her, saying that she was her niece, and she has left me papers that seem to prove that this is true. I'm keeping her anyway, because she was misused in that woman's clutches, and I'm adopting her. However, I have a good reason for wanting to know exactly what happened to her in Miss Gay's house—was ever a harridan worse named—and I want you to find out.'

'You say you got a reason,' said Bert slowly. 'Can you tell me what it is?'

'No. But it has to do with the murder I'm investigating.'

'What, the murder on the Ballarat train? You was on the train, Miss?'

'I was. And I've got the victim's daughter here, too. She has hired me to find the murderer, and so I shall. However. Find out all you can about dear Miss Gay. Who lives with her—especially men—who visits her, all of her background. Can you do it? Usual rates,' she added.

'The question is not, can we do it, but will we do it,' observed Bert. 'What do you think, mate?'

'I reckon we can do it,' agreed Cec, and Bert put out his hand.

'We're on,' he said, and Phryne poured them a beer to celebrate.

◇◇◇

Phryne took a nap that afternoon, and passed a quiet evening playing at whist with Jane and Miss Henderson, who had greatly recovered. Her blisters were drying, and Dr. MacMillan had hopes that her liver was not damaged after all. Jane showed an unexpected ruthlessness, and won almost seven shillings in pennies before they broke up and went to bed. Jane took Ember with her, as usual, and he slept amicably on her pillow.

◇◇◇

Lindsay Herbert lunched at the 'Varsity, went to his Torts lecture where he learned more than he thought that he needed to know about false imprisonment, and went home to dine with Alastair, who seemed subdued. His outburst in Phryne's house had profoundly shocked him, and when the young men had stacked the dishes in the sink for Mrs. Whatsis to clean in the morning, he lit a nervous cigarette and tried to expound.

'I don't know how to apologize to you, old man, for that appalling bad show at Miss Fisher's.'

'That's all right, old fellow, think no more of it.' Lindsay was sleepy with remembered satiation, and disinclined to listen to self-pity or even explanations.

'But it's not all right. I lost my head completely—just like those fellows in the Great War—shell-shocked, they used to call it.'

'Why, what shocked you?'

'First there was Eunice—poor girl, her face is all burnt, she looks dreadful—then you taking up with Miss Fisher and just wafting off without a word—then a policeman had the infernal nerve to ask me—me!—where I was on the night of the murder.'

'Well, I could scarcely say, "sorry, old boy, must rush, I'm being ravished by a beautiful lady", now, could I? Especially if I wasn't sure if she was going to ravish me or not. I mean, a fellow would look a fool, wouldn't he? And I suppose the police chappie has his job to do. Where were you, anyway?'

'Here,' snapped Alastair, butting out his cigarette as if he had a grudge against it. 'Did she?'

'Did she what?'

'Ravish you?'

'Old man, since the beginning of time, few men have been as completely ravished as I have been.'

'Hmm,' grunted Alastair. 'Are you seeing her again?'

'Friday night.'

'Well, ask her how she is going on the murder. She's taken possession of my fiancée and my friend, but she won't solve the murder by sex-appeal. No, Miss Fisher,' commented Alastair savagely. 'Not as easily as all that.'

'Well, well, I'll ask her,' said Lindsay peaceably.

'If you can spare the time,' snorted his friend, and stalked out to go to bed, slamming the door.

Chapter Ten

*'Then two are cheaper than one?' Alice said
in a surprised tone, taking out her purse.*

*'Only you must eat them both, if you buy
two,' said the Sheep.*

*'Then I'll have one please,' said Alice... 'They
mightn't be at all nice, you know.'*

Alice Through the Looking Glass,
Lewis Carroll

Bert and Cec found the large and imposing house at Railway
Crescent, Seddon, without much difficulty. It was in a fine state
of studied disrepair. The iron lace which decorated the verandah
was both unpainted and broken, and the bluestone frontage had
been whitewashed by some past idiot. The distemper was now
wearing off in flakes and tatters, and no maintenance had been
done on the roof since the Father of All was a callow youth. The
gate sagged on its hinges, the front garden was a wilderness of
hemlock and slimy grass, and the bell-pull, when pulled, emitted
a rasping screech and fell off in Bert's hand.

A sign had been painted over the whitewash next to the door.
It said 'Rooms to Let. Full Bord' in red lead. Bert had an idea.

'Quick, you get down the path, Cec, and I'll ask for a room. I don't want her to see you.'

Cec caught on and retreated into the bushes, and a scatter of footsteps announced that someone was coming.

The door creaked open on unoiled hinges, and a small and slatternly girl answered, 'What do you want?'

'I want a room,' rejoined Bert roughly. 'The missus at home?'

The girl nodded, knotting an apron stained with the washing up of several years, and swung the door wide.

'Come in,' she parroted tonelessly. 'It's ten shillings a week, washing extra, and no drink or tobacco in the house.' In a small voice, she added, 'But you'd be better to go elsewhere.'

Bert heard, grinning, and patted the girl on a bony shoulder. 'I got my reasons,' he said portentously, and the girl's eyes lit for a moment with an answering spark.

'What's yer name?' asked Bert, and the small voice said, 'Ruth. Don't let her know I been talking to you.'

There was such an undercurrent of fear in her voice that Bert did not reply aloud, but nodded.

'Who's at the door, girl?' demanded a screech from the back of the house. 'I don't know, girls these days can't do a good day's work, not like it was when I was a girl. Twelve hours a day I used to work, and hard, too. Now they snivel and fall ill if they're asked to serve tea. Well? Who is it?'

'Please, Missus, it's a man,' faltered Ruth. 'He wants a room, Missus.'

'Oh does he? Have you told him about it?'

'Yes, Miss, I told him.'

Ruth's eyes implored Bert not to say anything critical, and he began to feel a strong sense of partisanship with this overworked skivvy. Poor little thing! The woman was evidently a tartar.

'Yair, she told me. So, have you got a room or haven't yer? I ain't got all day.'

Miss Gay emerged from the kitchen, wiping her hands on a dirty teatowel. Bert looked her up and down and classified her instantly as Prize Bitch, filthy class. Prize bitches came in two classes, the fanatically clean, who smelt of bleach, and the slatternly, who smelt of old, boiled cabbage. Miss Gay was also redolent of yellow soap and sour milk. She was not a prepossessing sight, clad in down-at-the-heel house slippers, a faded wrapper in what appeared to be hessian, no stockings and a yellow cardigan draggled at the hips. Bert smiled his best smile and was rewarded with a slight softening of the rigid jaw and mean, thin lips.

'Here's me money,' he offered, handing over a ten-bob note that vanished into the unacceptable recesses of her costume. 'Show me the room.'

The small maid accompanied them up the unswept stairs to a room which had once been fine. The ceiling was high and decorated with plaster mouldings, and the walls had been papered with Morris designs. A plasterboard partition had been erected, cutting off the window, and the room contained a single iron army cot with two blankets, a dresser which had originally come from a kitchen, still equipped with cup-hooks, a table with one leg shorter than the others and an easy chair so battered that its original form could hardly be guessed. Bert concealed his loathing and said easily, 'This'll do me, Missus. What about meals?'

'Breakfast at seven, and lunch at twelve, if you come home to it. Dinner at six. If you want a packed lunch, tell me the day before. Put anything to be washed in that bag and it goes out on Monday. Washing is extra.'

'Latch-key,' suggested Bert, and one was detached from Miss Gay's jingling belt and handed over.

'No alcohol or tobacco in the rooms, and lights out at ten. No women, either. Visitors are to stay in the parlour. Board is due every Friday, at twelve noon, sharp. Anything you want, ask Ruth here. She's a stupid, worthless girl, but I can't abandon my own flesh and blood.'

Ruth twisted her dirty apron around a grimy hand and gulped back a sob. Miss Gay sailed away down the stairs, and Bert felt in his pocket.

'Here, take this,' he whispered, pressing half-a-crown into the girl's chapped hand. 'And not a word to a soul, eh?' Ruth nodded. Her brown eyes were bright and shrewd. 'You ain't one of her usual lodgers,' observed Ruth curiously. 'What are you doing here?'

'Go downstairs and get a broom and sweep this floor,' ordered Bert in a loud voice, and Ruth scurried down and returned with an article which could technically be called a broom, though it had scant three bristles left. With this, patiently, for she was a diligent girl, Ruth began to sweep the floor, while Bert explained what he was doing in a fast undertone.

'There's this girl, see, her name is Jane Graham. The Hon. Phryne Fisher has got this Jane in her care, because she's lost her memory—I mean, Jane has. Your Miss Gay turned up there this morning and demanded Jane, saying that she was her niece. Now my Miss Fisher reckons there is something wrong, and she sent me to investigate it. Do you know Jane?'

'Yes. She's my best friend, Jane is. She was here for about six months, after her grandmother died. First her mother died and then her grandma, and her father's a sailor, and he ain't never come back from his last voyage, so Missus took Jane.'

'Out of kindness?' asked Bert artlessly. Ruth laughed, a small slave's laugh.

'Kindness? Her? You're joking. She took Jane like she took me, for the work she could get out of us. But Jane was funny.'

'How, funny?'

'She had nightmares,' said Ruth. 'See, her grandma hanged herself, and Jane found her, in this house, it was, by the window upstairs, I durstn't go there. Then there was the mesmeric man.'

'The who? Look out, she's coming back. Hookit, Ruthie,' warned Bert, and shoved the girl out of his room.

'Come back with a broom that sweeps,' he said roughly, and Ruth ran down the stairs, passing the Missus. Miss Gay slapped at her, but Ruth was quick, and the blow missed.

'Girls!' snorted Miss Gay. 'Everything all right, Mr....'

'Smith,' said Bert. 'Bert Smith.'

'I've brought your rent book, Mr. Smith.'

'Thanks. Send up that girl with a real broom, will you? There's plaster all over this floor—a man could break his neck.'

Miss Gay departed, and Bert shut the door. His room had no outlet except the doorway, and he felt stifled. At some time a leak had started in the roof, and water had trickled down the wall, leaving a great rusty stain like a grinning face.

'A real palace,' observed Bert sardonically, and sat down gingerly on the army cot to wait for Ruth.

It was half an hour before she returned, this time with a reasonable broom, and she had been crying. Bert observed the marks of tears on the child's face and said, 'She been knocking you about?'

Ruth nodded.

'She told me not to talk to you, but I'm going to,' she said defiantly. Bert shut the door and leaned on it, occluding the keyhole in case Miss Gay should decide to eavesdrop.

Ruth took the broom and began to sweep noisily, and Bert asked, 'What was this man?'

'The mesmeric man, the hypnotist. On the halls, he was. At the Tivoli. He tried to hypnotize me, but I just pretended. He mesmerized Jane lots of times. He could make her think that ice was a red-hot poker, and after he touched her with the ice a red blister would form on her arm. He made her think that she was talking to her grandma, and telling her how the missus beat her, and then the missus would punish her when she came round. It was horrible,' confessed Ruth, sneezing in the plaster dust. 'But I was glad it wasn't me.'

'He still here?' asked Bert, shocked, and Ruth nodded.

'He's her fancy man,' she said gravely. 'That's what the lodgers say. He's got the best room and the window and all, and he gets all the good food—bacon and eggs and rolls and that.'

'You hungry?' asked Bert. 'Where did she get you?'

'From the Orphanage. I'm *not* her flesh and blood! She adopted me. My parents are dead. I wish she hadn't,' said Ruth sadly. 'I liked the Orphanage. The nuns were letting me teach the younger kids their ABC. I didn't want to leave, but she took me…There,' she added in a loud voice, 'I've swept up all the plaster, Mr. Smith.' Ruth's hearing, sharpened by pain, had picked up the approach of Miss Gay before Bert had heard her. He opened the door, and Ruth went out, carrying the broom and the dustpan. Bert emerged into the passage.

'I'm just going out for a couple of hours, Missus,' he said flatly, and walked down the stairs and out at the hall door. Bert felt that he had been dipped neck-deep in sewage.

He found the cab, with Cec in it, around the corner in Charles Street, and Cec started the engine.

'To the pub,' ordered Bert. 'I never, in all my born days, saw such a place as that. It's filthier than a pigsty and God alone knows what would happen to a girl.'

'So, we don't go back,' said Cec, stopping the cab outside the Mona Castle, and Bert shook his head.

'Oh, yes we do,' he said grimly. 'Something nasty is going on in that place, and I'm going to get to the bottom of it.'

'What was Miss Fisher not telling us?' asked Cec, when they had glasses in their hands, and Bert rolled another smoke.

'I don't know, but I'm beginning to guess, and I don't like what I'm thinking, Cec, I don't like it one bit.'

Bert told Cec what he was thinking, and they bought another beer.

'So I've taken a room there, Miss,' reported Bert on the pub telephone. 'And I gotta go back tonight. I want to meet this hypnotist chap.'

'Yes, you do want to meet him,' agreed Phryne. 'But be careful, won't you? They sound like very unpleasant people.'

'So am I,' growled Bert, baring his teeth. 'Me and Cec is very unpleasant people, as well.'

'All right, my dear, but keep in mind that I want to know all about the man before you pulp him. You have guessed about Jane, haven't you?'

'Yair Miss, I guessed. As soon as I heard about the mesmerism.'

'So I want him alive,' said Phryne urgently. 'He might be able to give her her memory back!'

Bert reluctantly accepted the justice of this.

'All right, Miss, I see what you mean. Me and Cec will be gentle with him. And there might be another waif, Miss. Orphan called Ruth. That bitch don't treat her right—beg pardon, Miss.'

Phryne sighed. Suddenly her life seemed to have become over-populated.

'Oh, well, one more won't make any difference, bring her along. When?'

'Termorrer, Miss, if we can manage it, and you might have your tame cop standing by.'

'Perhaps,' said Phryne, and Bert felt a chill go through his spine, the remembered over-the-top thrill.

'All right, Miss, I'll see you then, goodbye.'

He hung up, paid the publican for the call, and returned to Cec.

'She said that we can take the little girl as well,' he commented. 'Your shout, mate. No alcohol allowed in me new place of residence.'

◇◇◇

Phryne stared at the photograph which had been delivered. Had this man mesmerized Gabrielle Hart? It was time that Miss Hart was found. She would go to see Klara in Fitzroy.

◇◇◇

Bert went back to Miss Gay's house, and found that dinner was on the table. Cec had returned to their own lodging house to explain Bert's absence to their excellent landlady.

The dining vault was as cold as a Russian military advance and not as well provisioned. The great table, which was made of mahogany which had not been polished in decades, was laid with a spotted off-white cloth and a harlequin range of dishes. Quite of lot of them were cracked or chipped, and the silverware was Brittania metal and not clean. Bert observed that one place was set with clean, new dishes and real silver, and in front of it was the cruet, the bread, and the butter.

The five other occupants of the house were already seated. They seemed a forlorn collection, with all the spirit crushed out of them by a combination of life, circumstances, and their landlady. Bert thought of his own Mrs. Hamilton, all dimples and a dab hand with pastry, and envied Cec his dinner. Two old men, vague and possibly senile; a young man in the last stages of consumption, who was as thin as a lath; a labourer or small tradesman with a missing arm, who seemed to retain some individuality; and a sleek and roly-poly gentleman in spotless evening costume, waistcoat and white tie and probably evening pumps, though Bert did not look under the table. His manicured plump white hands cut the bread and buttered it as though there were no starving men at the same table. He had brown eyes like pebbles and that thick, pale skin which speaks of too much greasepaint at an early age. Miss Gay came in, bearing a tureen of frightful soup (which the gentleman did not take) and Bert was introduced.

'This is Mr. Smith,' announced Miss Gay, dispensing pig swill. 'Mr. Brown, Mr. Hammond', she said gesturing at the old men, who made no sign—'Mr. Jones' to the young man—'Mr. Bradford' to the tradesman, who nodded and spooned up his soup as though he was used to the taste. 'And allow me to introduce Mr. Henry Burton.'

'I saw you once,' commented Bert, pinning down an elusive memory, 'on the Tivoli. You were on the same bill as that Chinese magician, the one who used to catch bullets in his teeth.'

Mr. Burton bowed.

'The Great Chang; he died, poor fellow, doing that bullet trick, a few years later.'

Miss Gay served what smelt like a tasty chicken soup to Mr. Burton, from his own small saucepan. The other lodgers lacked the spirit even to glare at this arrant favouritism. Mr. Burton had a wonderful voice; rich, deep, persuasive, a vocal instrument perfectly wielded. Bert remembered the act which he had seen; a man behaving like a chicken, a woman stretched stiff as a board between two chairs. It had been very impressive. What was the great man doing in a dump like this? Surely he could not dote upon the appalling Miss Gay?

Ruth came in to remove the soup plates, and to hand out dinner plates, which were also mismatched and chipped. Miss Gay brought in congealed gravy, fatty, depressed roast beast of some sort—Bert suspected horse—and potatoes as hard as bullets. The lodgers munched their way uncomplainingly through this detestable repast, while Mr. Henry Burton dined on a pheasant in redcurrant jelly and winter broccoli.

Pudding was a floury suet thing with very little gooseberry jam. Even the old men could not eat it. Mr. Burton had water biscuits and stilton cheese. Bert drank a cup of hot water in which three tealeaves had been steeped and went up to bed. Most of the lodgers did the same. Bert reflected, as he lay down in the creaking cot, that he had been more comfortable on the hills among the dead men and the Turkish snipers.

◇◇◇

Phryne dismissed her taxi in Gertrude Street and emerged into the cold, wrapping her furs around her and snuggling her chin into the sumptuous collar of red fox. She was uncertain as to where she should begin in this rough place, in search of Gabrielle Hart.

She had a photograph of the girl. She looked again on the thin, unsensual, plain face, beaky nose and deep eye-sockets, a generous mouth. This young woman was not pretty, and would be consequently easy to seduce by flattery. She was sixteen.

By arrangement, Phryne met the unsettling Klara in a tea and sly-grog shop on the corner.

'Phryne! Come and buy me some tea,' called Klara. She was a small, thin woman dressed in a gym slip. Her hips and breasts had never developed adult curves; she looked like a pre-pubescent schoolgirl. She was twenty-three, lesbian, and very acute.

Tea was purchased. Phryne liked Klara, but found her company worrying. No one hated the whole male sex, absolutely and without exceptions, like Klara. She was a very successful whore, and her tax returns usually came in above three thousand pounds a year.

The tea-shop was cold. Klara was wearing only her gymslip and a ratty overcoat; her skinny legs were bare and muddy. Phryne huddled into her coat.

'Aren't you cold, Klara? Have some of this disgusting tea.'

'Oh, I'm cold all right, but that's what the punters pay for, ain't it? I'll be warm enough when I get home. Show me the photo.'

Klara drank the luke-warm tea and considered.

'I ain't seen her, but that don't mean she ain't here. We'll start at the end of the street and work our way down. Lucky it's such a crook night; no one'll be out pounding the pavements if they can avoid it. You equipped for trouble, Phryne?'

Phryne nodded. Her little gun was loaded and in her pocket.

'All right. Come on, love. Bye, Jack!'

A figure shining with grease looked up from the chip fryer and grinned.

'This is the first. The other two only deal in chinks. Hello, Alice. Got a friend with me tonight. Seen this girl?'

'Hello, Klara,' said the big woman in purple satin uneasily, shooting a sidelong glance at Phryne. 'No, I ain't seen her, she ain't one of mine.'

A languid girl, wearing only a stained silk petticoat, looked in on the mistress.

'The gent in number four is passed out,' she said casually. 'Better call the boys and put him out. I don't like his breathing; he's gone purple and is puffing like a grampus. Hello, Klara! What are you doing in this abode of vice?'

'Hello, Sylvia. Looking for this girl.'

Sylvia pushed back a mop of bleached curly hair and considered Phryne.

'You don't look like one of them Soul Rescue people,' she commented. 'What do you want her for?'

'I want to take her home,' said Phryne. 'Her father is worried about her.'

'Jeez, I wish I had a father to worry about me.'

'Do you know her, Syl?'

'Is there a reward?'

'There might be.' Klara consulted Phryne with a look.

'Yair. Well, she's the new one in Chicago Pete's. Better watch out, Klara. They ain't nice people. Saw her this arvo. Seemed dazed. She ain't been there long. Chicago Pete's girls always look like that.'

'Drugged?'

Syl shrugged admirable shoulders under the drooping silk. 'Maybe.'

Phryne folded a five-pound note and thrust it into Sylvia's hand. She and Klara regained the street.

'Chicago Pete?'

'Yair. A yank. They say he was a gangster, but they'll say anything on this road. Come along, there's the entrance.'

Phryne and Klara lurked, surveying the respectable darkstone entry of a two-storey house.

'How do we get in? And can we get her out?'

Klara grinned, showing unexpectedly white teeth between blistered lips. She felt in her shabby pocket and produced a knife.

'Even Chicago Pete knows not to muck about with me,' she hissed. Phryne wondered what elemental force she had let loose on Gertrude Street and decided that Gertrude Street could look after itself.

'Which way shall we go in?' asked Phryne.

'Front door,' decided Klara, and led the way up the respectable stone steps to a thick, closed door.

On this she knocked what was evidently a coded series of taps and it creaked open. A flat-faced individual was behind the door and stared unspeaking at the guttersnipe and Phryne in her furs.

'Well?' he asked in an American rasp.

'You new?' asked Klara scornfully. She came up to his second waistcoat button.

'Yeah, I just got off the boat, why?'

'I'm Klara, get Chicago Pete for me, willya?'

'Now why should I do that?'

'Because if you don't know me, Pete does, and he'll knock your block off if he misses me; we're pals, Pete and me.'

The doorkeeper let them into a well-kept hall and lumbered off up the stairs.

'Pals?' asked Phryne, noticing that the street-side windows were barred.

'Yair, pals. He says I remind him of his little sister. He's as queer as a nine dollar bill, Pete is. Here he comes. Gimme that photo and let me do the talking.'

Chicago Pete was a ruin; huge, damaged. His face might originally have been comely, but it had been beaten and twisted out of true as though an angry child had wrung a wet clay head between temperamental fingers. His eyes were dark, and as flat and cold as a slate tombstone.

'Klara! Why haven't you been here for a week, little Miss?' The voice was lovely, soft and rich with a Southern accent.

'I been busy,' said Klara. 'I got a proposition for you, Pete, and I want to do you a favour.'

'Come in here.' He ushered them into a room which was frilled and shirred in pastel shades, like a Victorian boudoir. 'I know you don't drink, little Miss, but I have lemonade. And maybe a good Kentucky bourbon for your friend, eh?'

Phryne accepted a glass and Klara sat on the edge of a table, exhibiting her thin legs splashed with mudstains. They affected Chicago Pete strangely.

'Why don't you wear some of them nice clothes I bought you, Missie? You make me sad, looking so bare.'

'Business,' snapped Klara. 'Listen. We want to buy one of your girls. This is my friend Phryne; she's acting for another party, and we don't want no trouble.'

'Which one?'

Klara handed him the picture. Chicago Pete's eyes narrowed. 'Her? You can have her. The cook reckons she's under a spell.'

'What, that black monster in your kitchen? What would he know?'

'You mind your tongue, Miss. The doctor, he's a New Orleans man, a jazz-man, a voodoo priest. He knows a spell when he sees one. She ain't worth nothing, that doll. And I paid…'

He stopped, calculating what the market might bear. Phryne smiled. She did not mind what she paid. Mr. Hart could afford it. And she was interested in the spell.

'Dope?' she asked, and Chicago Pete shook his awful head.

'No. Or if it is, it ain't like no dope I've ever seen. I'll get them to bring her down. Wait a moment.'

He stepped to the door, gave an order to the doorkeeper, and said to Phryne, 'She ain't been used much. And she ain't been damaged. Much. What will you offer?'

'How much did she cost you?'

'Ten bills.'

'Twelve.'

'Twenty.'

'Fifteen.'

'Nineteen. Here she is. Say hello to the nice lady, doll.'

The girl was limp, her gaze vacant. She was dressed in a nightgown far too big for her and her feet were bare. She was bruised over all of her body that Phryne could see.

'She must have had clothes,' commented Phryne. 'Can someone bring them? We'll dress her again, and then I want to see your jazz-man.'

'If you want him, he's in the kitchen. But I don't think…' Klara pointed, and Phryne went out, past the doorkeeper, into the back of the house where she could smell cooking.

'Shrimps and rice and peas,' said the thin black man, pointing into a pot. 'Very nice. What you want, Miss?'

'I want you to take the spell off Gabrielle Hart,' said Phryne, and repeated it in French. The old man grinned and took off his apron, then reached for a cloth bag and a handful of feathers.

'We had *poulet Orleans* for dinner.' He took a little dish that seemed to be full of blood. 'You know voodoo?'

'A little. I have been to Haiti. Can you do this?'

'*Oueh*,' he grunted. 'You pay me ten silver florins and I do it. Little doll will remember.'

'Who put on the spell? Another voodoo priest?'

The old man shook his head.

'Ain't none of my magic, but strong magic. Strong,' he repeated, hefted the loaded tray, and followed Phryne into the pink-and-blue sitting-room.

The girl had been clad in her own street clothes again, and Klara had combed her tangled hair and plaited it. She looked now like the schoolgirl she had been when someone snapped his fingers and told her to follow. Her eyes were still glazed. Klara had planted herself on Chicago Pete's knees and he hugged her very carefully, as though she might break.

'I don't like this,' he said uneasily, and Klara patted his cheek.

'It's worth nineteen bills, Pete,' she soothed. The priest set down the tray, and stared at the girl, then picked up her wrist and allowed it to drop.

'Strong magic,' he commented, setting out the blood and the feathers and laying down a white tablecloth over the Chinese carpet. He removed his shirt and began to anoint himself with the blood, muttering under his breath. Gabrielle stared at him. Her attention had been caught, for the first time.

Around the old man's neck swung a bright gold coin. Her eyes fixed on this as he began to dance.

Three times around the girl the old man moved; then he lit the bundle of feathers and cried out, 'Erzulie! You captured this soul! You possessed this girl! Erzulie! You took her! I call for the third time, and you release her. You give her back to the world: Erzulie!'

Neither Chicago Pete nor Klara had moved. The smoke from the chicken feathers filled the delicate room with a farmyard reek. Phryne almost fancied that dreadful, elemental things moved and squeaked in that smoke; she shook herself and pinched the back of her hand hard.

Gabrielle Hart flinched as from a striking thunderbolt and began to wail. Klara ran to her and hugged the shocked face against her skinny bosom. The old man straightened up, shiny with sweat, and held out a bloodstained hand to Phryne.

She poured the coins from her purse, and added one extra.

'You come on a Saturday,' he said to Phryne as he bent to collect the instruments of his magic. 'We got good jazz. Best in the city.'

'For the love of Mike,' cried Chicago Pete. 'Get out of here! And take all that heathen stuff with you!'

The priest folded the tablecloth and went out. Klara released the girl.

'All right, Mr., er…here is the money, and we must be going. Can your doorman call us a taxi? Thank you so much,' said Phryne graciously.

The doorman was dispatched for a cab. Gabrielle Hart sat in her chair and cried and cried.

'You sure you want her?' asked Chicago Pete, and Phryne smiled.

Klara and Phryne left the respectable house and waited for the taxi on the front steps. Gabrielle had stopped crying and was now asking questions, some of which Phryne could answer.

'What am I doing here? Who are you? Where am I?'

'I am the Hon. Phryne Fisher, and this is Klara. You are in Gertrude Street, Fitzroy, and only God knows what you are doing here. You had a brainstorm, my dear, and we are taking you home.'

'No, no, someone else said that to me…someone else said that they were taking me home…and they didn't…they *hurt* me!'

'Oh, Lord…all right. Calm yourself. You shall tell the driver where to go. Oh, thank God, it's Cec.'

Cec smiled his beautiful smile from the driving seat of the taxi.

'I'm on me pat,' he told Phryne. 'Bert's still about that...er... business with the boarding house. Poor old bloke. They said you was out on a case in Gertrude Street and I thought...'

'You thought right. This young woman is Gabrielle Hart, and she will tell you the address. Take her there and deliver her into the care of her father only. If he isn't home, wait, but I think that he will be there soon. Give him my card and tell him I shall call on him tomorrow. Hang on to this girl, Cec, don't let her get out until you are at her house. She's a little disordered.'

'All right,' agreed Cec, opening the door. 'Come on, Miss.'

Gabrielle Hart moved to the taxi, got in, and gave Cec the direction. He looked over at Phryne.

'What about you, Miss?'

'We'll get another taxi. She's scared of us. See you later, Cec.'

'We might as well walk down to the rank,' suggested Klara. They had only gone about three paces before the attack came.

Two men came quickly, out of an alleyway. They disregarded Klara, brushing her aside, and both grabbed for Phryne. She dropped to her knees under their weight; she heard her stocking tear and felt her knee graze. They had one arm each, and she could not reach her pocket. They did not say a word. Phryne's breath scraped in her chest. They were taller and heavier than she.

A Master-at-Arms had once spent three weeks teaching Miss Fisher the elements of unarmed combat. She was not afraid, only very angry that she should be taken thus off guard. She allowed her fury free rein.

'Crack' the first one's knee as she kicked back, hard, then rammed her high-heeled shoe down on his other foot. He let go. With the impetus from that Phryne flung herself at the other attacker. Her elbow caught his ribs; her knee came up with all her force, and he fell to his knees, dropping a cosh. Phryne, fast and lethal, retreated a pace and kicked again, and felt a rib or two break with a curious, dry sound.

'Bastards!' panted Klara, standing on the other attacker's stomach with one foot on his throat. 'Pete musta changed his mind about the girl.'

'No, not Pete, I think.'

Phryne kicked over one man and dragged his head up by the hair.

'Who sent you?' she hissed. The man looked up glazedly into blazing green eyes and winced.

'Who?'

Phryne shook him and bashed the skull against the ground a few times. 'Tell me or I'll kill you.'

The knife was at the attacker's unsavoury collar. He blinked.

'I just reckoned you'd be rich, dressed up like that,' he croaked, and fell out of consciousness.

'Fitzroy is so bad for the nerves,' sighed Phryne. 'Leave him alone. I owe you a good dinner and a night out, Klara. What shall it be?'

'The Bach concert on Tuesday, and dinner at the Ritz,' decided Klara. She dusted off her hands and pulled down her gym tunic. 'I prefer Johann Christian, but I can put up with Johann Sebastian. We can get a taxi at the rank. You all right, Phryne?'

'Fine,' agreed Phryne, pulling up her torn stocking. 'I'm fine.'

Chapter Eleven

*'Give your evidence,' repeated the King
angrily.*

*'Or I'll have you executed, whether you are
nervous or not!'*

Alice Through the Looking Glass,
Lewis Carroll

Phryne woke on Thursday morning knowing who had murdered Mrs. Henderson, and wondering what she was going to do about it. The method was obvious, the motive transparent, and even the face of the blond guard was beginning to resemble one which she had seen in real life.

'How shall I do this? It will break poor Eunice's heart.' Phryne took her morning bath without appreciating the scent and dressed in haste.

It had to be Alastair Thompson. He was used to disguise. He had a terrible temper. He had no alibi for the night in question. All that he had to do was to chloroform the people, sling a rope around Mrs. Henderson, and cast a line over the water tower. He was a rock climber. Then he could haul her up, and himself, and leave no tracks. Whether he dropped her or trampled on her did not matter. All he had to do was to get rid of the mother and

Eunice would fall into his arms and give him all her money, of which Phryne supposed that there must be a fair amount.

Phryne decided to call Detective-inspector Robinson, and when she had established contact with him, found that he had reached the same conclusion.

'I'm bringing him in for questioning today,' he assured Phryne. 'I'm of the same mind, Miss Fisher. I'll let you know.'

Phryne decided that there was no need to worry Miss Henderson with any news until she could say something positive, and closeted herself with her solicitor, who had drawn up the adoption papers.

'But Miss Fisher, you have kept the girl from her guardian's care,' he protested. Phryne grinned and shoved Miss Gay's 'documents' at him.

'She has no legal guardian. Miss Gay is her aunt, but no adoption proceedings were ever taken. Here's her birth certificate and all. Poor little thing. Have you sorted it all out?'

'Yes, Miss Fisher. If you will just put your finger on this seal and repeat after me, "To this adoption I hereby put my name and seal"—just a legal form, Miss Fisher, you understand—and it is all completed.'

Phryne complied.

'She's mine, now?'

'After the judge has approved this, yes.'

'Excellent. When can you get it into court?'

'In due course, Miss Fisher.'

'That won't do. "In due course" means at least six months.'

'It is a practice court application, so I can probably get it into the list for next week,' said the lawyer, shocked yet again by Miss Fisher's disrespect for the law. He bundled up his papers and took his leave. Jane tapped at the door of the parlour.

'Miss, I've recalled something.'

'Good. What is it?'

'I remember Miss Gay. She took me and Grandma to her house. It was a horrible place. Grandma...something happened to Grandma.'

'It will come back. Nothing more about the train?'

'No. Was that your lawyer, Miss Fisher?'

'Yes. I just signed the adoption papers. You're mine now, Jane, and no one can take you away.'

Phryne told herself that she should have known better than to say things like that. Jane began to weep, threw herself at Phryne and held her tight, and Ember scratched his way onto her upper arm, balanced like a small black owl, and glared.

'You are quite right, Ember,' Phryne told him. 'It was a very silly thing to say. Never mind. Jane, my dear, here is a hankie, and I think that we should sit down. All this emotion is wearying, isn't it?'

◇◇◇

More emotion was expressed by a horrified client on the telephone.

'Miss Fisher, I must first thank you for retrieving my daughter.' He began with deceptive calmness. 'But do you know what they have done to her, those hounds?'

'I have a fair idea,' admitted Phryne. 'She has certainly been beaten.'

'Beaten, and…and…assaulted, and the doctor thinks that she may have a…venereal disease.'

'Yes.'

'Who were they?' he screamed. 'Tell me their names!'

Mr. Hart dropped any pretence of control.

'I don't know their names, and if I did I should not tell you. Private vengeance is unsound, and moreover illegal. Leave them to me.'

Some nuance in her voice must have told Mr. Hart that he was talking to a very angry woman.

'You know them?'

'I shall know them. And they shall all be very, very sorry. I promise.'

'Is there anything I can do?' asked Mr. Hart, subdued.

'Nothing. They have ravished your daughter, and a thousand offences beside. Leave them to me. Your daughter needs you now. She is an innocent victim, poor thing. She probably won't remember anything about it, so don't remind her. I am sure that you can find her the best of care. Then take her right away from Melbourne for six months. Switzerland has some very pleasant scenery.'

'I put my confidence in you, Miss Fisher.'

'So you may, Mr. Hart.'

She hung up the phone. How was she going to find the abductor and avenge poor Gabrielle Hart? But now she was determined. She had given her word.

◇◇◇

Detective-inspector Robinson surveyed the young man in the clutch of two policemen with approval. He was a fighter, this one, and it had taken the combined strength of four officers to bring him in. Even now he was straining in the grip of the station's two heaviest and strongest officers.

'It is my duty to warn you that you do not have to say anything, but that anything you do say will be taken down and may be used in evidence,' he said quietly.

The prisoner demanded, 'What are you charging me with?'

'The murder at or near Ballan on the night of the 21st of June 1928 of Anne Henderson by strangulation,' said the policeman, and Alastair Thompson laughed.

'Then you've got another thing coming. I'll tell you where I was on the night of the 21st of June 1928.'

'Well, I'm glad that you have decided to tell me at last.'

'I was in the City Watchhouse,' sneered Thompson. 'Drunk and Disorderly. I was fined five bob the next morning. Cheap at the price, considering. Go on. Ask the watchhousekeeper!'

This was a surprise. Detective-inspector Robinson, however, preserved his habitual calm.

'Book him in, please, Duty Officer,' he requested civilly, and the young man was forced into a chair to be photographed, stripped of boot-laces, tie and braces, and placed with a certain celerity into a nice quiet cell.

'Get those developed and send across for the drunks book,' he snapped, and an underling carried off the camera and raced across the road to the Watchhouse, demanding the Cell Register for the 21st of June.

'You can't have it,' snapped the sergeant. 'It's my current book and I need it. Tell Jack Robinson to come and inspect it himself. What's all this about?'

'Murder suspect says that he was banged up on the night,' gasped the cadet. 'He'll skin me if I come back without it! Have a heart!'

'You can copy the page,' said the sergeant, relenting. 'And you can note at the same time the names of the officers what were on duty on the night of the twenty-first. Who was it?' He leaned ponderously over the counter. 'Aha. Sergeant Thomas and Constable Hawthorn. You can have Hawthorn, for all the use he is, but you can't have Thomas, he's on leave.'

'When will he be back?' asked the cadet, scribbling furiously with a spluttering pen on the back of a jail order. 'This nib is frayed, Sarge, I swear.'

'He's in Rye on his honeymoon,' replied the sergeant, grinning evilly. 'Didn't leave no address. There you are, son, and take Constable Hawthorn with you. Hawthorn!' he bellowed.

A faint voice echoed from the cells, 'Yes, Sarge?'

'Get across and see if you can identify a prisoner of Jack Robinson's, will you lad? And you needn't hurry back. Get some lunch.'

'But sarge, it's only half-past ten!'

'Get some breakfast, then,' snapped the Sergeant, and the cadet conducted Constable Hawthorn back across Russell Street to the detective-inspector's office, waving his jail order the while so that the ink would dry.

The cadet peeped up at Hawthorn. He was very tall, over six feet, and pale, and vague. His mouth had a tendency to drop open and his eyes had the dull, unfocused gaze which the cadet had previously only seen in sheep.

Hawthorn asked mildly, his voice as bland as cream, 'What's this all about, young feller?'

'Please, sir, the detective-inspector has a suspect for the Ballan railway murder, and he says that he was in the Watchhouse that night.'

'And he wants me to identify him?'

'Yes, sir.'

'Oh,' remarked the tall constable, and accompanied the cadet to Robinson's office.

The copy was laid down on the desk and Robinson scanned it irritably.

'You read it, boy,' he snarled at the cadet, and the boy read, 'John Smith, 14 Eldemere Crescent, Brighton.'

'He's an old customer...name really is John Smith, too, and no one ever believes him—has to carry his birth certificate around with him. Says he's never forgiven his father for it...no, that ain't him. Go on.'

'John Smith, The Buildings, East St. Kilda.'

'Now I don't know that one. Do you recall that John Smith, Hawthorn?'

'Yes, sir. About...er, well, smallish, and er...fair, with...er... blue eyes, I think, sir.'

'Could you identify him?'

'Oh, yes, sir,' said Hawthorn. 'I think so.'

Detective-inspector Robinson grunted, got to his feet, and led the way to the holding cells. A furious face glared up at the window-slot as he drew back the bolt.

'Have a look, son. Is that the man?'

'Oh, yes, sir,' agreed Hawthorn happily. Robinson gritted his teeth, and gave the order to release the suspect from detention.

'I didn't want to tell anyone that I'd got drunk, so I gave a false name. I believe that this is not unusual. May I go now?' asked Alastair, with frigid politeness.

'You may go, but you are on bail. You may not leave the state or change your address without notifying us of your where-abouts. Do you understand that?'

'I understand,' said Alastair, with a smile that showed all his teeth, and he turned and left the police station.

Detective-inspector Robinson lifted the telephone and requested Miss Fisher's number.

'I don't think that it's disastrous, but it certainly casts a lot of doubt on my theory,' said Phryne when the exasperated policeman reached her. 'Have you examined his handwriting? He would have had to sign himself out. And are you sure of the police witness?'

'No, Miss, that I am not. Boy's a fool. However, identification is identification.'

'Wasn't anyone else there?'

'Yes, but the sergeant is on his honeymoon, I can't call him back.'

'No, but you can send him a photograph, can't you?'

'Yes, I'll do that. And I'd keep out of Alastair's way, Miss Fisher, if I were you.'

'I can look after myself,' said Phryne crisply. 'Get weaving with the photo. See you soon,' she added, and hung up.

The cadet was very impressed that the detective-inspector could swear for so long without repeating himself.

◇◇◇

Bert in later years said that breakfast at Miss Gay's was the single most miserable experience of his whole life. 'Not sad, mate,' he explained. 'But down right starving mean stone the crows and starve the lizards dirt miserable.'

The table was laid, as before, with cruet and mismatched plates, and Mr. Henry Burton's special dishes.

They sat in a hungry circle around a vat of horrible porridge, as thin as library paste, scorched, and lumpy, while Mr. Henry Burton said grace in an unctuous voice. Bert refused the clag, but the others ate voraciously. Mr. Burton was breaking his fast on new rolls, hot from the oven, cherry jam, and butter. He had a pot of brewed coffee next to him. Bert accepted a plate of incinerated egg-powder and bacon so burned as only to be of professional interest to a pathologist. He tried to make a sandwich with his two pieces of stale white bread and marge, but the bacon broke as he touched it with the knife.

'Can't you give a man a feed?' asked the tradesman, holding out a plate on which reposed a four-days-dead egg and bacon of transcendant carbonization.

'I can't take your bacon back to the kitchen, Mr. Hammond,' snapped Miss Gay, slapping at Ruth's head as she passed. 'You've bent it.'

Bert drank a cup of tea and chuckled.

After breakfast, the workers departed, and Mr. Burton showed signs of going out. He took his hat and his stick, donned a fleecy-lined overcoat, and yelled for Ruth.

'Call me a cab, girl.'

Bert grabbed the moment.

'I'll get you one, sir,' he said civilly, and stepped into the kitchen, where Miss Gay kept the telephone.

'Ruthie!' he whispered, 'we're taking Mr. Burton. Here's a card. You go to this house if she hurts you again.'

Ruth nodded, stowed the card in her pocket, and Bert slipped back into the hall.

'At the door in a moment, sir,' he said, and went down the rickety front steps to look for Cec, who was due directly.

The bonzer new taxi pulled up, and Bert opened the door for the gentleman, closed it and jumped into the front seat.

'Here!' protested Mr. Burton, 'I didn't ask you to share my taxi!'

Bert grinned.

'It's my taxi—well, half mine. This is my mate, Cec. Say hello to the nice gent, Cec.'

Cec muttered 'hello' and kept his eyes on the road.

'Where are you taking me?' asked Mr. Burton.

'A lady friend of ours wants to see you real bad.'

'Which lady?'

'The Honourable Phryne Fisher, that's who.'

'Is she a fan? I hope that she does not want her fortune told. I don't tell fortunes, you know.'

'No, she wants some mesmerism done,' said Bert.

They were on Dynon Road and fleeing like the wind for St. Kilda. If he could keep this oily old bastard talking, that would be all the sweeter.

'Yair, some of that hypnotizing what you done on the Halls, they say you used to be great.'

'Used to be? My dear sir, I am the Great Hypno. You yourself have seen my powers.'

'Yair, I remember. You made sheilas as stiff as boards and laid 'em between two chairs. But I don't reckon you could put anyone under that didn't want to be,' said Bert easily, and Henry Burton bristled.

'Oh no? You, for instance?'

'Yair, me, for instance.'

'Look into my eyes,' said Henry Burton, 'and we will see. Look deep into my eyes.'

Bert looked. The eyes, which were brown and had seemed hard, were now soft, like the eyes of a deer or a rabbit; deep enough to drown in. They seemed to grow bigger, until they encompassed all of Bert's field of vision; the voice was soothing.

'You hear nothing but my voice,' said Burton softly. 'You hear nothing but my words, my voice, you do nothing but as I command you. You cannot move,' he suggested softly. 'You cannot lift your hand until I tell you.' Bert, terrified, found that he could not lift his hand. He was frozen in his half-turned position, seeing nothing but the eyes, and wondering vaguely why he could not hear the engine of the cab or any other noises. Bert began to panic and vainly struggled to move so much as a finger.

Cec stopped the cab outside Phryne's house and got out. He opened the door and commented in his quiet, unemphatic tone, 'If you don't release my mate, I'm gonna break your neck.'

Mr. Burton flushed, leaned forward, and snapped his fingers in Bert's face. 'You feel rested and refreshed,' he said hurriedly. 'You are awake when I count ten. Ten, nine, eight, seven, six, five, you are free now, four, three, two, one. There.'

'Just a demonstration,' said Mr. Burton airily, and got out of the car and climbed the steps to Phryne's front door.

Chapter Twelve

*'It's time for you to answer now,' the Queen
said looking at her watch. 'Open your mouth
a little wider when you speak…'*
    Alice Through the Looking Glass,
        Lewis Carroll

'Ah, this must be the Great Hypno!' exclaimed Phryne, as Mr.
Butler conducted her guests into the parlour. 'This is my companion Miss Williams, and we are delighted to meet you. Do
sit down. Would you care for a drink?'

The Great Hypno smirked and bowed, gave his coat and hat
to Mr. Butler and took a seat, accepting a whisky and soda.

'You wanted to see me, Miss Fisher? What about, may I
inquire? It must be pressing, since you had me kidnapped. I am
pleased that my fame is still strong, I have been retired from the
stage for five years.'

'Yes, why did you retire? Bookings not too hot?'

The man bridled, tugging at his glossy forelock. 'Certainly
not,' he said indignantly. 'I found another…er…line of work,
which was so engrossing that it required me to devote all my
time to it.'

'Yes, I have always thought that it must be a tiring profession, procuring.'

Bert, who had remained near the door, nodded as though he had had his suspicions confirmed. Cec watched the scene with a still face, but his fists clenched.

'You take the likely ones from orphanages,' stated Phryne. 'And the repulsive Miss Gay adopts them. Such a charitable woman! I've spoken to three institutions where she is well known. A lady with a social conscience, they said, those stupid people, a lady who takes on the hard cases and bad girls and finds them suitable employment. That is with the help of her tame mesmerist, who makes sure that the difficult ones don't raise any dust. Eh, Mr. Burton?'

'I have never been so insulted in my life!' huffed the stout man, fighting to get out of his armchair. Phryne laughed.

'Oh, come now, in all your life? You mustn't have been listening. Don't get up, Mr. Burton,' she added, revealing the dainty gun which she was aiming at him. Mr. Burton blanched. He dropped back into the chair and extracted a silk hankie and mopped his face.

'Come on, admit it and don't waste my time!' snapped Phryne. 'Or I shall have an accident with this little gun, you see if I don't! How many girls? Talk!'

'It must be…oh…thirty-five or so. Yes, thirty-five, if you don't count Jane.'

'Thirty-five,' said Phryne stonily. 'I see. Where did you sell them?'

'Various places. I supplied the country, mainly. They mostly came from the institutions well broken in, you know, little tarts in all but profession, and it wasn't necessary to hypnotize many—a waste of my Art, as I told Miss Gay. All it generally needed was to explain the situation, that they were going to make a lot of money, from something more pleasant than domestic labour, and most of them agreed.'

'And then what?'

'When the girl was in the correct frame of mind, we would arrange for her journey, wiring ahead to the buyer.'

'How much did you ask for each girl?'

'One hundred and fifty pounds. Good girls, most of them. Though I only got a hundred for that little bitch from the Emily MacPherson. Of course there was a certain wastage—always is in that profession—suicide, alcohol and drugs, mainly, and of course venereal disease, but all I sent were clean and relatively new, my buyers know that.'

Phryne swallowed. Dot stared, open mouthed. Cec reached for the nearest decanter and took three deep gulps, passing it to Bert. Mr. Burton, full-fed and shiny, sat back, amused by their reaction.

'Why are you so shocked? It is your nice society which demands that there should be whores and there should be nice girls. While there are nice girls there must be whores—all that I did was supply them.'

'Being a whore should be a matter of choice,' said Phryne. 'And what choice did you give them? Did you ask Gabrielle Hart if she wanted to be raped and drugged? Now, Mr. Burton, I have a proposition for you.'

'I thought that you might have,' smiled Mr. Burton.

'You remember Jane?'

'Yes, whining little scrap, with her books and her Ruthie and her grandma.'

'Yes. Jane. You hypnotized her, did you not?'

'I did. She was on the train to Ballarat to join a very exclusive house there, run by a generous friend of mine, but she never got there. I put her on the afternoon train, and she was found on the night train. She must have got off somewhere, but I can't explain what went wrong—she had explicit post-hypnotic instructions.'

'I want you to give her back her memory,' said Phryne quickly.

'And if I refuse?'

'Then I fear…' said Phryne, waving the little gun. Mr. Burton observed that her attitude was negligent and her purple silk afternoon dress positively decadent, but her wrist did not droop and her finger was on the trigger.

'Bring her in,' he said, coughing into the handkerchief. 'I will try. But she may not respond. I tell you, there has been another intervening event, a trauma of some sort.'

'Did you always have sex with the girls, Mr. Burton?' asked Phryne.

He answered absently, 'Oh, yes, Miss Fisher, it was part of the treatment, and part of the reason why I stayed in the business. There have to be some compensations for retiring from the stage. But this one, I recall, squealed, and then I recalled that the Ballarat brothel paid a fifty pound bonus for virgins, so I relented. I didn't like to hurt them, you know.'

Bert made a choking noise and wrung his felt hat to ruin. Phryne gave him a severe look.

'So the trauma was some other thing, not a sexual assault?' asked Phryne evenly.

'Oh, yes, something quite unexpected,' said Mr. Burton, unconscious of any irony. Dot went out and fetched Jane, who came in warily, not knowing Mr. Burton but not liking him, either. Phryne concealed the gun, and took the girl's hand.

'Jane, dear, you sit down here and look at this gentleman. You are quite safe. I am here, and I will not leave you.'

Ember stalked off Jane's shoulder and onto Phryne's lap, curled into a fuzzy black ball and purred. Jane relaxed. Mr. Burton leaned forward, placing one thumb on her forehead.

'You are sleepy, Jane, are you not?' The magnificent voice was as deep as organ music. 'Are you asleep, Jane?'

Jane's eyes were open, but her voice was cold and character-less, like the voice of a ghost. 'I am asleep.'

'What were this man's commands to you?' asked Phryne, and Jane twitched a little at the unfamiliar voice, but answered: 'To forget what he did to me.'

'Jane, that command is removed,' said Mr. Burton, eyeing the pistol barrel within a foot of his face. 'You are free and released from all commands, from me or anyone else. From the time that I count from ten you will begin to remember, and by midnight you will recall everything that has happened. Do you understand, Jane?'

'I understand that I am free,' repeated the mechanical voice, and even in deep trance it had a different quality. 'I understand that I am not under your command anymore.'

'Ten, nine, eight, stretch yourself, Jane, seven, six, five, four, blink, girl, you feel rested and refreshed and you will recover your memory slowly until at midnight it will be complete, three, two, one, awake!' He snapped his fingers in Jane's face, and she blinked, focused, and drew back into Phryne's embrace with a cry.

'It's him! The man who…hurt me. He scratched at the window and made me let him in. Oh, Miss Fisher, don't let him take me away!'

Phryne hugged Jane, and then transferred her to Dot, while Mr. Burton stood up and smiled his satisfied smile. Dot clutched a frantic Jane and was scratched by a frantic Ember, who blamed her for being dislodged from Phryne's knee.

'Well, Miss Fisher, I have done what you wanted, shall we discuss payment?'

Cec growled, and Bert took two steps forward.

'Payment?' he shouted. 'You filthy hound, I'll break your bloody neck!'

'One moment,' said Phryne, holding off Bert with a gesture. 'Are you willing to give yourself up to the police?'

'Really, Miss Fisher, are you joking? And if you let your hired ruffian lay a finger on me, I'll have an action for assault and battery. I am going to walk out of that door a free man, Miss Fisher. Do you know why? Because not one of those thirty-five would testify against me. They all love me like a father, the little fools, and in any case seven of them are dead.'

'You are *not* going to walk out that door, do you know why?' asked Phryne, smiling unpleasantly, 'because there is a rat in the arras. Did your shorthand writer catch all of that, Jack?'

'Yes, Miss, got it all down pat,' said the detective-inspector, stepping out from behind the curtain. 'I bet you weren't expecting to see me again, eh, Henry?'

'Robinson!' gasped Henry Burton. 'How did you get here?'

'I've had you on suspicion for years, you bastard,' The detective-inspector smiled his sweetest 'come-along-with-me' smile. 'I've got the testimony of nine of those little girls, once their trance wore off, but it wasn't enough, as there were great gaps in their memory. They couldn't remember how they got into the grips of a portly, respectable gentleman with beautiful eyes. Now I know that Miss Gay got 'em from the asylums, it won't be too tricky to connect it all up so that even my chief will have to believe it.'

Bert and Cec seized the Great Hypno.

'Just one punch,' pleaded Bert. 'Just the one.'

'No, I gotta get him back to headquarters. He's a mine of information. He knows all about the vice rings and all the white slaving in Victoria. I don't want him damaged!'

Diving under the arms of the struggling men as quick as a bird after a worm, Jane launched herself out of Dot's embrace and flew at Mr. Burton, fingers hooked into claws. She was mad with release and the intolerable rush of returned memory, and Ember, springing from her shoulder, clawed at whatever foothold he could reach as Cec restrained the struggling child and hauled her away from the ruin of Henry Burton's face.

Ember fled to Cec, as all cats did, and tucked his small spade-shaped head in the crook of the tall man's arm. Jane, her fury spent, buried her face in his shoulder, and he held her head down so that she should not have yet another horror to burden her memory.

Razor-sharp, kitten claws scrabbling desperately for a hold had done what no poor twelve-year-old whore had managed. They had dimmed Henry Burton's magical gaze.

Shocked, Bert released the man, and Mr. Butler, who had been an enthralled spectator throughout, telephoned for an ambulance. The room was silent, except for Jane's sobbing and the muted bubbling snuffle of Burton, who had clamped his hands over his face. The ambulance came in ten minutes, during which time no one moved or spoke, and Robinson and his shorthand writer and his prisoner went away. The front door shut. Still no one moved. Cec stroked the kitten and Jane with equal gentleness, and Dot drew a deep breath and stood up.

'Well, that's all over, and a very nasty end, and you can't say that he didn't deserve it, the horrible man. Mr. B., ask Mrs. B. for some tea, will you? Miss, you might like a brandy? Mr. Cec, can I offer you a drink? A cup of tea?'

Her brisk voice brought everyone to. Phryne rummaged for a light for her cigarette. Jane sat up and wiped her face on Cec's shirt. Bert sat down and rolled a smoke with hands that hardly shook at all. Cec smiled up at Dot.

'Thank you, Miss, I'd like a beer, and so would Bert, and then a feed. Poor bloke's been living on cabbage stalks and offal for days.'

It is an index to how much better they were all feeling after a few minutes that when Ember removed his head from the crook of Cec's arm and began to wash his front feet, no one shuddered at the thought of what he was washing off.

'Mate, mate, we was forgettin'!' exclaimed Bert, slamming down an empty beer glass. 'What about little Ruthie?'

'She's in the kitchen,' observed Mrs. Butler tartly, refilling the glass with ease and skill. 'She's been here for ten minutes, but I couldn't interrupt you. Such goings on in a lady's house! But it all seems to be over now. Ruth is well, Mr.…er…Bert. She says that Miss Gay beat her again, and she has a beautiful black eye, poor mite—and she ran away to Miss Fisher like you told her. She's in the middle of a bath, or I'd call her in. Is this horrible business settled, then?' she asked in a worried undertone, but not low enough to escape Phryne. Mrs. Butler moved aside to allow Jane and Ember to rush to the kitchen. Cries of delight greeted them from the Butler's bathroom.

'This particular horrid business is over,' she said, patting her housekeeper on the arm, 'but the other horrid business is sent right back to square one. The person that had all the earmarks of being the murderer on the train has the best alibi of all—he was in police custody, so that puts him right out of the picture. Dear me. What a tiring day! Can you manage an early dinner, Mrs. B.? Poor Bert has been on a reducing diet lately. Then I think that we could all profit from an early night. Tomorrow I'm going with Miss Henderson to open up her house and help her clear out, and Dot and Jane are coming too. That will be exhausting enough, but then I've just remembered that the students' Glee Club is on at the boathouse tomorrow night.'

'Yes, Miss, an early dinner, I've got some fish that the boy swears was caught this morning, and I can easily make a few extra chips. Will that suit? And don't worry about your problem,' soothed Mrs. Butler, seeing that Phryne was white and strained. 'It will quite likely solve itself if you don't worry at it. More beer, Mr. Bert?'

Bert held out his glass and grinned.

'It's worth a man doing a perish if he gets one of your dinners, Mrs. Butler.'

'Go on with you,' sniffed that lady, and bustled back to her kitchen to fry up a storm.

Jane was sitting on the hearth, with a scrubbed-clean Ruth. Ember was on her lap. The kitten had quite recovered and was watching the flames with his ears laid back as though he was at his mother's breast.

'I'm remembering a lot more,' she said quietly. 'I remember getting off the train, at a station in the middle of big open paddocks. I didn't know who I was or where I was going but I knew that I didn't want to go there. I sat down on the station seat, then it got dark and a train stopped, and I heard a child crying, so I went to get him and I put him on the train again, then it seemed silly to stay where I was, so I got on the train too, and hid in the ladies. I stayed there until…something happened…then I was at Ballarat and I couldn't remember a thing. It feels like it happened to someone else, not me,' she explained. 'All cotton-woolly, as though it was a movie.'

'And, of course, there was no one on the station to meet you, because you were on the wrong train,' mused Phryne. 'It all fits, Jane.'

Jane looked up suddenly and laid a hand on Phryne's silk-clad knee. Her upturned face was very young.

'Am I still a good girl, Miss?'

Phryne, leaning down to embrace Jane with an unaccustomed catch at the heart, assured her that she was.

Chapter Thirteen

…and she was quite pleased to find that there was a real one blazing away as brightly as the one she had left behind.

'So I shall be as warm here as I was in the old room,' thought Alice.

'Warmer, in fact, because there'll be no one here to scold me away from the fire.'

Alice Through the Looking Glass,
Lewis Carroll

'Lord, isn't it cold in here? Never mind, Dot will soon have a fire lit. Did you have any servants, Eunice? If so they haven't left the old place in any sort of order.'

'No, I dismissed them, with notice of course, and I fear that they haven't complied with their employment conditions.'

Phryne, Dot, Jane, and Ruth had escorted Eunice Henderson to her home in case she should be overwhelmed by her memories as she climbed the front steps to the dull grey door. When it became clear that Eunice had a grip on her emotions they turned to the more pressing matters an unoccupied house presented them with.

The house had that musty chill which falls upon unoccupied houses, and depresses the spirits of all visitors. Dot hung up her good blue coat on the hallstand and went to find the kitchen, taking the girls with her, to light the stove and open some windows. Dot carried her capacious basket well supplied with a picnic, and tea and sugar and a bottle of milk. Phryne helped Eunice out of her coat and elected to remain wrapped in her sables.

Eunice ran a glove along the hall table and examined her finger; it was coated with dust. The house was an elegant Edwardian family mansion, stoutly built and ornately decorated, but it was unloved, overcrowded, and dilapidated. Phryne picked up a vase in which lilies had died; they moved with a sad rustle in their slime-green water.

'This will need an army of parlourmaids to set in order,' sighed Eunice. 'When are your cleaners coming, Miss Fisher?'

'I told them ten o'clock, and that will be them now, I expect. Admirable women; Mrs. Butler recommends them.'

Phryne answered a strident ring at the bell and ushered in a small stout woman and a small thin woman, relieved them of their coats, and pointed them toward the diningroom.

'There you are, ladies, I suggest that you make a start by opening all of the windows and letting a nice fresh gale in. Miss Henderson, this is Mrs. Price and Mrs. Cummings.'

'Glad to meet you, ladies,' said Eunice. 'Do you think that you can manage? It's a frightful mess.'

The thin woman tugged at her hem, tied her apron strings, and wrapped an enormous red and white bandana around her head.

'Me and Maise'll manage,' she said. 'Done worse than this, eh, Maise?'

Maise nodded, enveloping her head in a blue scarf.

'Hot water in the kitchen?' asked Adela Price, and Phryne nodded. They squared their shoulders.

'I'll do the windows, Dell, and you open the flues and start the fires,' said Maise, and Eunice led Phryne upstairs.

'I'm afraid that it has all gone downhill since Mother lost all her money,' she apologized. 'She used to be very well-off, you know, and she got used to luxury. It was all that I could manage to keep her in linen sheets, after the crash of the Megatherium Trust, you know.'

'Your mother had money in that trust?' asked Phryne, catching up on a dusty landing and following Eunice into a dark bedroom. The Megatherium Trust, a hastily put together fraud perpetrated by the Honourable Bobby Matthews, remittance-man of Phryne's acquaintance, had crashed resoundingly at the end of May 1928, taking all its investors with it. The Hon. Bobby had elected to seek the warmer and less indictable climes of South America. Phryne had not been sorry to see him go. Megatherium indeed! Many less-than-funny jokes had been made about prehistoric monsters after the crash.

'Oh, yes, all of her money was in Megatherium. She lost every penny that she had. Dear me, this carpet is sadly motheaten. Do you think that your friends will want such a sad relic?'

'Bert and Cec can find a home for everything, even if it's only the tip. Pardon me for asking, Eunice, but does your young man know this?'

'Why, no, the question never came up. I suppose that he assumed that I was wealthy. I am well provided for, of course, but entirely by my own labours.'

'Oh?' asked Phryne, her mind buzzing with theories, 'what labours?'

'You promise not to tell anyone at all?' pressed Eunice, stopping with an armload of dreadful dresses.

'Not a soul,' promised Phryne, crossing her heart.

Eunice opened a little door and slipped inside. Phryne had taken it for a powdering closet, but it was a study. There was a professional looking typewriter and a load of carefully numbered manuscripts. Phryne remembered the packet of foolscap paper she had picked up in the train.

'You're a writer!' she cried. Eunice Henderson blushed.

'Romantic novels for railway reading, and, dear, they are too, too terrible.'

'What are you working on at present?'

'Nothing at the moment, I have just been correcting the proofs of *Passion's Bondslaves*. It is quite the most disgusting drivel I ever read, so I am sure that it will be just as successful as *Silken Fetters* and *Midnight of the Sheik*. I sold a thousand copies of that in two weeks, and it's still in print. You won't tell, Phryne, will you?'

'Of course not, my dear, but I think that it is so enterprising of you! How did you begin?'

'Well, Mother always liked to read the things, revolting slop for the most part, and I learned typewriting so that I could do Mother's accounts. I was practising on the machine, and I thought I'd see if I could write the stuff, it seemed easy enough, and, my dear, it simply poured onto the page, I could hardly type fast enough to keep up. I never knew that I had such an indelicate imagination,' she confessed, throwing down the dresses in a rustling heap. 'So I sent it to a publisher who knew my father and could be sworn to secrecy, and there it was. I can write one every three months, and the market seems rather under-supplied with tripe than otherwise. So I could afford lavender-water for Mother, and handmade chocolates, and trips to Ballarat, and...oh, dear, I had forgotten all about Mother! How heartless of me!'

Eunice sat down on the brass bed and wept for five minutes, at the end of which she wiped her eyes, replaced her handkerchief, and went on with the conversation.

'It will catch me like that for awhile, now that my face is healed and I'm not doped with pain-killers,' she said sadly. 'Poor Mother! Who could have killed her?'

'For a while I thought that it was your young man, Eunice, God forgive me,' confessed Phryne, sorting shoes into a pile. 'But it can't have been him.'

'It can't?' she asked tautly.

'No, it seems that he was in police custody that night. Drunk and Disorderly.'

'How...how very unlike him.' Eunice flung three gloves onto the pile. 'I have never seen him touch alcohol...at least, very rarely. Never mind. I forgive your suspicions, Phryne, it did look black against him. Why did Mother keep seven unmatching stockings, do you think? What are we going to do with all this stuff?'

'We are going to put all the clothes and so on in a big heap in the upstairs hall, and Dot will sort from there. Some of the things will go to deserving causes and the worst will be dropped off at the rag-pickers by Bert and Cec. All we have to do is to decide what you want to keep.'

'All the stuff in here can go, and this carpet—it will probably roll if you can dislodge the corner...thank you.' They began to carry out a motley collection of old clothes, good clothes, handbags by the hundred, shoes ranging from the Victorian to the Edwardian, combs and boxes of caked powder, greasy hairpins, mob-caps and lacy petticoats. After two hours they had sorted out all the upstairs rooms and Phryne was ready for a cup of tea and a cigarette.

Dot, Ruth, and Jane were working at the clothing mound, packing the good things into teachests and the rags into chaffbags. Bert, Cec, and the charwomen were removing the discarded furniture, knick-knacks, what-nots, and so on into Bert's disreputable van.

'It really is lovely to clean out all this old rubbish,' said Eunice as they passed the workers on the way to the kitchen. 'But are you sure that anyone would want all this stuff? Look at that glass bowl over Great-Grandma's wedding bouquet! What an excrescence!'

Cec, who had earmarked the glass bowl as a present for his sweetheart, commented, 'Real good glass, this. Made by a craftsman,' and Miss Henderson smiled warmly.

'Take it and enjoy it,' she recommended.

Cec grinned.

Bert called from the door, 'Are you coming, mate? A man hasn't got all day!' and Cec grabbed the glass dish and went.

Phryne and Eunice had their cup of tea, and surveyed the sterling work which had already been done. The floors were swept clean, the windows open, the fires burning, and the house smelt pleasantly of wood smoke and furniture polish.

'It is very kind of you to help me, Phryne,' she observed. 'This will all be finished in one day, and I can sleep in my own bed tonight.'

'You won't mind being here on your own?'

'No, dear, what could harm me? I am exorcising the ghosts of all of my family, and I shall be quite happy alone. I'm only keeping the basic furniture, and all of those ornaments and feathers and dead birds and seashells and small tables can go. I am throwing out the firescreen made by Aunt Matilda, whom I always hated, and dear Cousin Nell's *petit point* chair, and Uncle John's butterfly collection. It's a fine empty feeling,' she continued, a little intoxicated by all that space. 'It's a nice house, if it wasn't all cluttered. And the curtains. I have always hated those heaped up lace curtains.'

'Don't throw them away, you need something to cover the windows,' objected Phryne. 'Cut them off.'

'Cut them off?'

'Yes, just snip them level with the floor.'

Eunice Henderson flung herself at Phryne and kissed her soundly.

'Oh, Phryne, why did I never think of that? In all that time when I hated the idea of all that lace lying around on the floor for the sole reason of demonstrating that you could afford to have lace lying on the floor, and I never thought of that! Quick! Where's the scissors?'

They snipped with a will, and the yards of superfluous lace joined a century's gleaning of costumes in the chaff bags. Dot claimed armloads of delicate undergarments for her own; Jane and Ruth found a store of satins from China and were allowed to keep them all; Bert took a fancy to a huge conch, and took it for a present to his landlady. It took eleven trips of the rickety van to various destinations before the detritus of seventy years was removed from the house, and Phryne marvelled that it still looked full. The linen room was bursting with Irish sheets, there were beds and tables and chairs and fire irons and paintings, but only one ornament remained in the entire mansion; a tall blue vase, quite unfigured, which some pirating ancestor had picked up in the Boxer wars.

'It's the only thing of Mother's that I wanted,' said Eunice, as they sat around the kitchen table sipping afternoon tea. 'I want you to have it, Phryne. It will go beautifully with your sea-green and sea-blue salon.'

'Oh, Eunice, I couldn't, it's much too valuable…'

'Yes, you could. Otherwise I shall break it. I don't want to see another ornament in my entire life. I shall have a study in the breakfast-room, which looks out onto the garden. I shall be very happy. And I am still employing you to find out who killed my mother.'

'Yes, I know, old thing, and I haven't the slightest idea at the moment. However, something will turn up. Are you sure you are all right to be left?'

'Perfectly,' asserted Eunice, as she stood bidding them farewell in her scoured, cold hallway. The wind had been from the west and the house smelled of the sea. Behind her in the swept-clean morning-room a bright fire glowed, and her supper was laid out on the one remaining small table. Phryne kissed Eunice goodbye, and allowed Bert to give her a lift home in the truck, in which she sat nursing the blue vase as though it was a child.

◇◇◇

Phryne dined early with Dot, Jane, and Ruth. Jane was preoccupied, and between the egg-and-bacon pie and the chops Phryne asked her what the matter was.

'I've remembered,' said Jane. 'What sent me off—what broke his power. It was something I saw. You know about my gran? She hanged herself, my gran did, at the window of the upstairs at Miss Gay's.'

'What did you see?' asked Phryne. 'Don't tell me if you don't want to.'

'I saw an old woman hanged,' muttered Jane. 'She was pulled out of the window by her neck; just like my gran's, her head was.' Jane's head flopped sickeningly sideways in demonstration. 'It was bright moonlight, like it was the night my Gran died. That's what set me off. That's why I went queer.'

'Where was this, Jane?'

'By the tower, the thing that the trains get water from. And there was a man there, Miss Fisher, a man.'

'What was he doing?'

'Pulling on the rope. The body rose, and so did he; he climbed over her and onto the water tower, then he swung her and dropped her on the grass. It was horrible, and I hid my eyes. Then he jumped down…'

Jane broke off. Ruth caught Jane in her arms.

'Ruthie! It was awful!'

'You just tell Miss about it,' commanded Ruth, and Jane obeyed.

'He landed on her body and…'

'I know what he did, Jane. No need to go on. Then what did you do?'

'I was watching out of the window of the ladies, Miss, and I heard a terrible scream behind me, and then the train started again. I just stayed where I was, Miss.'

'Would you know the man again, Jane?'

'Yes, Miss. I expect so.'

'Good. Now you and Ruthie sit down and eat some chops and let's get on with the dinner, for I am famished.'

Ruth paused with a fork halfway to her mouth and asked the question that had been concerning her since her arrival.

'Miss Fisher, what are you going to do with me?'

'I'm not going to do anything with you, if you mean by that, something to you. What would you like me to do?'

'Jane says that you are sending her to school.'

'That is true.'

'And that you like intelligent girls.'

'Yes.'

'And you adopted her.'

'Yes,' agreed Phryne, wondering what was coming.

'I'm intelligent and I can work hard and I have always looked after Jane. What'll she do without me? You should take both of us, Miss, not just pick one like kittens out of a litter.'

Jane laid her hand on Ruth's shoulder and looked at Phryne. Ruth bit the end of one plait reflectively. Then she took up her fork and swallowed the piece of chop impaled on it, as though she was not sure when she would get another meal. Phryne smiled.

'Two are better than one,' she said. 'I was wondering how Jane would manage in this rackety house on her own. All right, Ruth. You too. Any relatives?'

'No,' affirmed Ruth, and took some more bread, thankful for the first time in her life that she was an orphan.

'I'll call that irritating solicitor tomorrow and get it all put through legally. But you will have to go to school, girls, through term, and you can come back here in the holidays. You can do anything you like, as long as you are willing to work for it. And you must never say anything about my cases, nothing at all, do you understand?'

Both heads nodded. They understood. Ruth grinned a huge grin and slapped Jane on the shoulder.

'No more Miss Gay, Jane, no more Seddon, no more of the Great Hypno, and best of all…'

'Best of all?' asked Phryne.

'No more dishes,' concluded Ruth, and hugged Jane so hard that Ember scratched her.

◇◇◇

Phryne finished her dinner and went upstairs to change, wondering what she should wear to a Glee Club singalong. She decided on comfort, dark trousers and jacket, and her sheepskin overcoat, perfect for the chill, dark night which it promised to be.

She was coming downstairs when the phone rang and she picked up the receiver. It was Detective-inspector Robinson, evidently in an elated mood.

'Miss Fisher? Ah! Answering your own phone? This'll never do—I just rang to tell you about our scoundrel.'

'Oh? Which one?'

The policeman chuckled.

'Burton. He's out of hospital and helping us with our inquiries. He's singing like a canary, unlike that prize bitch of a wife of his.'

'What? Married to Miss Gay?'

'Indeed. The wounds to his eyes ain't serious—just scratches, but he seems to have lost his power. Tried mesmerizing one of my constables—you never had such a laugh in all your life.'

'Be careful of him, Jack, he's dangerous.'

'Miss Fisher, it's well known that you can't be hypnotized if you don't want to be. He's lost his fangs, all right.'

'His dentist will have to fit him with an entirely new set. Congratulations.'

'Thanks, Miss Fisher. And another thing, I got a reply from Thomas, you know, the sergeant down at Rye on leave?'

'And?'

'Can't say yes or no. Said he remembered the man, but couldn't say if that was him or not. Said it was an odd case—he didn't seem very drunk, but when the beat constable passed him by, he tripped him and then tried to steal his helmet. Young gentlemen will have their tricks, especially young university gentlemen.'

'Indeed. Well, that's about all that we can do at present. Oh, Jack, I forgot to tell you. I have an eyewitness to the murder, who saw what happened and can identify the murderer.'

'An eyewitness to the murder, Miss Fisher? Who?'

'Jane, I told you she had remembered. Listen.' Phryne told the story of Jane's grandmother and the manner of her death.

'It appears that the old woman hanged in a noose against a lighted window is what shocked the child out of the trance your harmless Mr. Burton had put her into, and she saw the man on the water tower.'

'She saw him?' exclaimed Jack Robinson. 'To know again?'

'So she says,' replied Phryne. 'I'll bring her tomorrow to look at photographs. All right?'

'Tomorrow,' agreed Jack Robinson.

Chapter Fourteen

'He had softly and silently vanished away…'
'The Hunting of the Snark,'
Lewis Carroll

Ruthie and Jane had so much to catch up with that Phryne suggested moving Ruth's camp-bed into Jane's room. She knew that they would talk all night but thought that they might as well do it in comfort. Jane was regaining her past in large chunks, and Phryne hoped that it would not prove too indigestible.

Ruth, Jane, and Ember partook of a light supper of bread-and-butter and hot milk, then they all snuggled into Jane's bed so that they could talk without being heard. It was a cold night, but the girls and the kitten were warm in their nest under the eiderdown with the jazz-coloured cover. Phryne looked in on them as she was going out.

'Good night, my dears,' she said, and heard the chorused 'good night, Miss Fisher' from the heaped covers. She smiled and closed the door.

'Dot, I'm going to this Glee Club do, only because I promised to bring the beer. Go to bed, old thing, and don't worry. Mr. B.! All the crates safely stowed?'

'Yes, Miss Fisher, all secure.'

'All right, I'm off—I may bring company home, but I shan't need you again tonight. Everyone can go to bed. We've all had too much excitement lately. All the locks and things up, Mr. Butler? Good. Well, sleep tight,' said Phryne, and sailed out into the night, a furry cap on her head, huddled in the sheepskin coat, and looking like a rather dapper member of the Tsar's entourage of female soldiers. She started the Hispano-Suiza without trouble, steered her carefully into The Esplanade, and turned her nose for the city. The wind whipped her face, tearing at her hair and she laughed aloud into the rainy dark. It was fine to be on the road with all this power at one's fingertips! She leaned on the accelerator, and the car leapt like a deer under her hand.

She rolled carefully down the unmade road to the boathouse, and it was obvious that there was revelry afoot. The boathouse, a rather rickety two-storey construction with a balcony, was lit with lanterns, as were several of the surrounding trees. There was a measured chorus of voices singing Blake's 'Jerusalem'. Phryne stopped the car and listened. It was perfect. The rain drifted softly down, the river ran with a slap and gurgle, and the voices, from highest sop to lowest bass, were blended as finely as a Ritz Hotel cocktail.

> Bring me my bow of burning gold
> Bring me my arrows of desire
> Bring me my spear, Oh! Clouds, unfold!
> Bring me my chariot of fire!

Blake really was an excellent poet, Phryne reflected, lighting a cigarette and leaning back on the leather upholstery, though regrettably mad, as poets so often are.

The song finished. Several people came out onto the balcony, and one girl exclaimed in a high-pitched voice, somewhat affected by gin, 'Oh, I say! What a spiffing car!'

'That must be Miss Fisher,' someone else commented. 'I hope she's remembered the beer!'

'I have remembered the beer,' she called up. 'But you'll have to carry it yourself.'

There was a clatter of feet, and several young men erupted out of the boathouse and down the steps.

'Oh, Miss Fisher, I'm so glad that you could come. Let me help you out, what an amazin' car! Very kind of you to bring some refreshments for the lads...and the girls, of course, I was forgetting. Connors, you and Tommy Jones get the beer, will you? Do you remember me, Miss Fisher?'

Phryne accepted the eager clasp and extracted herself from the driving seat, summoning up the name to match the bright, intelligent face.

'Of course I remember you,' she temporized. 'Aaron Black, that's who you are. Well? What about the bet?'

'You can call on me for a row down the river in a real boat,' he confessed, grinning. 'They know several much ruder songs than we have heard. But we are learning. We think that we should put the two societies together, Miss Fisher, I mean, silly, isn't it, in these days of equality, females all over the shop, I mean, women students in Medicine and even in Law; silly to have separate singing, when all parts in music are of equal value. What do you think of it?'

Phryne allowed herself to be led up the stairs by this charming young man, past a series of boats stored in racks like coffins, and up onto a plain dancing floor, with a servery in one corner and the balcony at the end.

'It's a bit of a crush,' apologized Connors, panting past with a crate. 'I always think that the balcony is not going to make it through another party, but it has managed so far.'

'Beer?' cried a huge young man, seizing the crate and extracting a bottle. He bit off the cap and gulped half the contents before his outraged friend regained possession.

'Beer!' he said with a delighted smile, and grabbed for the bottle again.

'Behave yourself, oaf! This is Miss Fisher, donor of all that amber liquid and some plonk for the ladies, so be civil.'

The huge dark young man took up Phryne's gloved hand with wincing delicacy and bestowed a respectful kiss.

'Madam, your kindness overwhelms us...can I have my bottle back now, Aaron?'

Aaron returned the bottle, seeing that Phryne was amused, and the chorus began on a sad tale of a young maid who was poor (but she was honest). Phryne sighted Alastair across the room, scowling, and the beautiful and diverting Lindsay near him, looking embarrassed. Then two young women claimed Phryne's attention and a bottle of her wine and she elbowed her way out on the balcony, where there was a wicker garden-seat.

'What do you think of this idea of putting the two societies together, Miss Fisher?' asked the blonde girl, gnawing at an ink-stained fingernail. 'They are pretty rough types, these Glee-ers.'

'Nonsense, Marion,' retorted her companion, who was thin and stylish and would be elegant when she started wearing stockings. 'They're nervous around us. Once they see that we aren't put off by the vulgarity they'll be all right. And we need some basses if we are to put on that B Minor Mass you're always talking about.'

'I suppose so. The world has a lot of men in it, doesn't it? It won't do just to pretend that they don't exist. Miss Fisher, we are devoted admirers of yours. We read all of your cases. Are you engaged in one at the moment?'

'Why, yes, I am engaged in the cases of the vanishing lady and the appearing lady; one died and one is alive.'

'Ooh, a riddle! Let's see if we can guess it. Do you want some of this wine? It's rather good,' said Marion. 'Let's get Alastair onto it, he's frightfully good at riddles.'

'Alastair!' shrieked the other girl, but Alastair did not seem to have heard her. He turned his back to the balcony and was arguing with Lindsay.

'What's wrong with him lately?' demanded Agnes. 'He's terribly shirty at the moment. Used to be a good enough chap, too, though a shark for the books.'

'I'm doing Arts,' explained Marion. 'Agnes here is doing Medicine. So is that Alastair chap, and he was rather fun, though over the last year he's been awfully dull. Does nothing but talk about money.'

Phryne accepted some of the wine, a good Traminer Reisling from the Hunter Valley which she had personally selected as being light and sweet enough for a student's taste. No glass being evident, she drank out of the bottle, sharing it with the two girls.

'I don't know that one,' remarked Agnes. 'What are the men singing?'

> Behind the door, her pappy kept a shotgun,
> He kept it in December and the merry month of May
> And when they asked him why the heck he kept it
> He kept it for a student who is far, far away

'Far away', carolled the tenors, 'Far away', growled the basses, 'He kept it for a student who is far, far away.'

'That's a good song, we must learn it. Look here, Agnes, I think you're right. It sounds much better with us all singing together. So much more balanced. Not shrill, like we used to sound.'

'Ah, and you should have heard us,' commented Lindsay from behind Phryne. 'We growled like bears with sore heads. Now the sound is quite perfect.'

'Not quite perfect,' disagreed Johnson, poking his head under Lindsay's arm. 'There is a lot of dissonance which can be removed by rehearsal. We need to knock the raw edges off and get used to singing in time with each other. Listen. One half of the room is out of tempo with the other half.'

This was true. Someone had started the old catch, 'My man Tom has a thing that is long,' which the girls also knew. 'My maid Mary has a thing that is hairy,' they replied, but somehow got irremediably out of synch, so it was hard to tell whose thing was long and whose thing was hairy. Eventually cacophony was reached and they broke off, laughing.

'Was that as indelicate as it sounded?' asked Phryne, and Marion blushed. 'It's a broom and a broom stick.' Phryne laughed and had another mouthful of wine. It was cold and dark outside, and the rain slanted down in sheets, but in the boathouse it was very warm, and the wine was delicious, and the singing was (occasionally) excellent. Phryne relaxed for the first time since she had left the bed with Lindsay in it and produced a flask of Cointreau.

This drink was new to many who tasted it, and it seemed to have a powerful effect. Edwards, the music student, suggested a negro spiritual, and they began to sing 'Swing Low, Sweet Chariot'. The battery of voices in that confined space, all trained to hit a note so that it went down and stayed down, was terrific. Phryne felt tears prick her eyes, as she joined in, and Marion was openly snuffling.

> I looked over Jordan, and what did I see?
> Coming for to carry me home
> A band of Angels coming after me
> Coming for to carry me home.

Before the impact of the song had time to die away, Edwards was pushed aside and the bespectacled madrigal enthusiast flourished a pile of sheet music.

'Sops on the right, basses on the left,' he ordered, and Phryne was left alone on the balcony.

She reclaimed her flask and sat staring out into the night, enjoying the rain, until she felt a hand slide up her calf to her knee and she covered it with her own.

'It's me, dear lady,' said Lindsay's voice from the floor, where he was lying out of sight of his fellow choristers. 'Have you forgotten me so soon?'

'No, dear boy, I haven't forgotten anything at all. Come and sit next to me, or do you like it there on the floor?'

'If they see me I shall be dragged off to sing—I like it better here—how smooth your legs are. Smoother than anything I can think of, except your thighs.'

'You are an impudent young man,' said Phryne, catching her breath. 'What were you quarelling with Alastair about?'

'Does it matter?' asked Lindsay, laying his head in her lap. 'Will you take me away and ravish me again tonight?'

'Perhaps, if you merit ravishing. What was the quarrel?'

'How tiresome you are, I shall be jealous of Alastair, you are so interested in him. If you must know, he wants to move out of my house, and he has packed up all his things. I was asking him where he was going to go, and he took me up uncommonly short and told me it was none of my business, which of course, it isn't.'

'When is he to go? Stop fooling, Lindsay, this is important.'

'Tomorrow,' replied Lindsay, hurt. 'I don't know where he's going but I think that it might not be unconnected with the not-so-blushing beauty and the money. Funny, you know, that was the night I spent in the jug.'

'You *what*?'

'Oh, I hadn't done anything wrong,' protested Lindsay. 'Old Alastair used to have spiffing ideas, you know, before he went strange.'

'Did he?' asked Phryne in a tone so compelling that Lindsay got up from the floor and faced her. 'What did old Alastair suggest?'

'Well, it was like this,' he stammered, staring into the face of a fury, cut out of marble, with eyes of green ice. 'He said that if I was going to be a lawyer I ought to understand about prisons, and the only way to really understand a prison is to be in one, and he said that I should get myself taken up for Drunk and Disorderly and be locked in overnight. Everyone gives a false name, you know. For God's sake, Phryne, what's wrong? What have I done?'

'Where's Alastair?' she asked through numb lips, and scanned the room; an easy thing, since Alastair should have been with the tenors, and he was not there.

'Come,' cried Phryne. She shinned down the verandah pole, leapt and raced for her car, with the young man behind and gaining fast. Phryne threw herself into the driving seat and jabbed the self-starter. The powerful engine turned over with a roar.

'Where are we going?' yelled Lindsay.

Phryne cried, 'We are going to prevent another murder—if we get there in time.'

Lindsay hung on as the Hispano-Suiza, howling on all cylinders, rocketed over the lumpy track and into the road.

Lindsay did not know that cars could go that fast. Phryne, when roused, could drive like a demon, having taken lessons from Miss May Cunliffe, the Cairo to London Road Race winner. Phryne had strong nerves and wiry wrists and the engine of the Hispano-Suiza had been built for racing. The rain drummed on the roof and the windshield; the lights smeared as though marked with vaseline.

Lindsay hung on, cheering, exultant; Phryne clutched the wheel and bit her lip and hoped that she had guessed where the murderer was going.

After ten minutes, Lindsay said, 'Phryne, we are going home, I mean, to your house, are we not? What do you think is going to happen there?'

'I don't know,' snapped Phryne, skidding around a slow trundling truck. 'Reach into the side pocket, will you?'

'My God, Miss Fisher, a gun?'

'Can you use it?'

'Yes,' agreed Lindsay dubiously. 'I've fired one before.'

'Good. Just try not to kill anyone with it. Now, listen. When we get to the house I want you to walk noisily down the left sideway, and I'll go down the right. Make a lot of noise. Sing, if you like. Be genial and drunken if he is there. Hold him until help comes. Can you do it?'

Phryne felt, rather than saw, the spine stiffen and the jaw harden. There was good stuff in the young man.

'I can do it. Why is he going to your house?'

'Because he's found out that Jane has seen him before.'

The car rolled to a silent halt in the cold street. Rain washed the cobbles and slicked the asphalt. Phryne buttoned her coat and pulled her cap down over her eyes, leaned over, and kissed Lindsay hard on the lips.

'Good luck,' she said, and got out of the car.

'Over the top,' said Lindsay, remembering a hundred woeful movies.

He tasted Phryne's kiss on his lips all down the dark alley at the side of the house.

Chapter Fifteen

'Somehow it seems to fill my head with ideas,—only I don't exactly know what they are! However, somebody killed something, that's clear, at any rate...'

Alice Through the Looking Glass,
Lewis Carroll

There were no lights in the house, and it was getting on for one in the morning. It was so quiet, except for the swish of the rain in the leaves, that Phryne could hear Lindsay on the other side of the house, singing in his pleasant tenor 'Swing low, sweet chariot' interrupted by the occasional hiccup. He really had a talent for acting, which his arrogant friend would never suspect. It was dark, and wet, and Phryne had not realized how many lumpy objects, just at shin height, were stored in her sideway. She banged into what seemed to be a spade, to judge by the clatter, and caught it up, using it to mark her steps and make as loud a noise as possible.

Perhaps she was wrong. Perhaps he had gone to call on Eunice, perhaps he had taken a female Glee-er into the bushes (though surely even students were not that lusty on a night like this), perhaps he had gone blamelessly home to bed. A branch struck Phryne across the face and blinded her; when she could see again she had been seized in a bone-breaking hold and there was a hand over her mouth.

She did not struggle, since this was futile; she gave a gasp and allowed herself to go limp. Her attacker was not expecting this; he had to change his grip to bear her up, and he grabbed her around the waist, leaving her hands and her mouth free. She was carried for a few paces, the strength of her captor surprising her. Phryne was a light weight, but this man carried her as if she weighed no more than a feather.

'Fainted, have you?' snarled a distorted voice. 'Miss fineairs Fisher, stealing my friend away like a poor dog to a flaunting bitch. I'll show you, Miss Fisher, who thinks you are so clever. Then I'll kill you, and leave you lying splayed for your lover to find. I can hear him, stumbling and singing, the drunken loon. Playing hide and seek, were you? First you, then him, then the little bitch, and the money is all mine.'

He dropped Phryne on her back and began to tear at the buttons of her sheepskin jacket. Phryne was cold with horror; the man was ten times stronger than she, and she had little time before she would be pinned like a moth.

Quickly, neatly, she rolled, drew up her legs, and kicked out with all her strength. She felt her heels sink into something soft. Her attacker gave a roar like a wounded boar and fell to his knees, catching Phryne's neck with his right hand. His agony was measureless, his grip like that of an ape, and Phryne tore at the fingers. His one hand was not wide enough to encompass her throat, but he had his thumb on the carotid, and the air began to redden before her eyes.

'Oh, there you are, Alastair, old chap,' burbled Lindsay, a little breathlessly. He had heard the shout and had broken the land speed record for running around houses in the dark.

'A fine night isn't it? Oh, I love these cool nights, to repose on the pale bosom of winter,' he carolled, lifting his full bottle, which he had found in the car. 'Have you seen Miss Fisher? Lovely girl. Oh, there she is.' He stared owlishly at Phryne's purpling face. 'Sorry, old chap,' he added, and brought the bottle down with all his force on his housemate's head.

The bottle cracked and broke, the scalp split, and blood blinded Alastair. He released Phryne, who crawled away, groping for the side of the house to haul herself to her feet.

'Alastair, are you dead?' asked Lindsay, bending low, and falling headlong as the strangling hands shot up out of the dark and fastened on his neck. He was dragged close to the blood-blubbered face, and did not have time even to cry out.

Phryne fired a bullet from the small gun and hit Alastair in the thigh. The body jerked, but he did not relax his grip. Lindsay thrashed, suffocating. Phryne raised the gun again and shot Alastair neatly in the forearm, disabling the wrist, so that she could pull the choking Lindsay away, and they stood embracing each other as the monster writhed on the leaf-mould.

'Go in, call the police, quick!' cried Phryne. 'Hurry!'

And Lindsay, coughing, stumbled away and she heard him pounding on the door. Lights went on in the hall. She could see the attacker clearly now. Alastair had been a good-looking young man; now he had the terror-mask of a beast, and Phryne retched when she looked at him. She held the gun unwaveringly, aware that it was glued to her hand with drying blood, and the moments crept on. More lights, and voices, and the 'ting' of the telephone taken off its hook. The thing on the ground stirred. Phryne backed, raising the gun.

'Kill me,' it muttered, blood bubbling from its nose.

'No,' she said, noticing that her voice trembled.

'Kill me. I wanted to kill you. I tried, and failed. It is the natural law. You must kill me.'

'No,' said Phryne. Her knees felt weak. If someone did not come soon, she would fall, and be within reach of that creature on the blood-spattered leaves.

'You killed the old woman,' she said, bolstering her courage.

'I did. She was useless. All women beyond childbearing are useless. She never trusted me, anyway. It was easy. I stole a uniform, got on the train, chloroformed Eunice and the old woman, then when the train stopped at the tower, I flung up my rope and a grapple, and there we were. She was no weight at all, really. And the power! I felt that I could rule the world. That's what murder does for you, Miss Bitch Fisher. It gives you the power of a god.'

'You came here to kill Jane,' said Phryne. 'She hasn't reached childbearing yet. Wouldn't that be a waste?'

Alastair heaved and thrashed, trying to sit up.

'Come and help me,' he demanded.

Phryne did not move.

'You're afraid of me, aren't you? And you should be. I am the superman.'

'I've heard of it,' commented Phryne.

'It would be a waste, but there is a lot of waste in nature. A million sperm to make one cell. A thousand little turtles hatched and only seventy reach the sea. Nature is prodigal. It would make more girls, and she had remembered. She was a danger to me...to me! No little tart could stand in the way of my destiny! All of those under protection shall flourish. All else shall be destroyed.'

'Eunice didn't flourish,' said Phryne, wondering if she had a fever or the night was getting hotter. 'You burnt her face.'

'A trifling error. I never used the stuff; it's old-fashioned, but I needed it because it is heavier than air, I wanted something that would drop down onto the faces of the sleepers. If you don't help me sit up, I'm going to choke on all the blood that is running down the back of my throat,' he added.

'Choke then,' said Phryne as Mr. Butler, Lindsay, and Dot rushed out of the house and she fell into Dot's arms.

'Better tell the cops to bring a doctor,' she gasped. 'Or his deathwish will be fulfilled.'

Dot bore her into the light, and Phryne caught sight of herself in the hall mirror. Her face was white, her eyes surrounded with black hollows, and there was no colour in her lip or cheek. She had, however, ample colour in the purple marks of fingers, so clearly delineated that Jack Robinson later suggested dusting her for prints. Phryne laughed at this, because they had taken away the unspeakable Alastair, strapped to a stretcher, raving, but alive, and she was contemplating a very stiff brandy and soda.

Dot had revived the parlour fire, and Lindsay cast himself down on the hearth rug and closed his eyes. He was smeared with leaf-mould and blood, and was as bruised as Phryne was, from the grasp of those terrible hands. Mr. Butler brought him a drink mixed to the identical recipe. When he had absorbed this and another, a little pink came back to his face and he was able to focus again.

He saw Phryne decorously divested of her jacket and trousers and dressed in a flowing woollen gown, grey-green as gum leaves, after Dot had sponged the mud and blood spatters from her face and hands. Lindsay was treated likewise by Mr. Butler, who washed his face as though he was five years old and still unreliable with chocolate. He gave up his tweed jacket, damaged (he feared) beyond repair, and his smeared trousers, and assumed a dressing-gown and slippers. He was back in his place before the fire, newly washed and dressed, feeling as he had when he was a child, and his nanny had brought him into the drawing-room for an hour before dinner.

Phryne cradled a steaming cup of strong black coffee in both hands, and Lindsay took his with a bewildered thankfulness, as though he had been woken out of a bad dream. A sip taught him that it was Irish coffee made with very good whisky. He drank a little, wondering why his throat was so sore, then became aware that Phryne was telling a story.

'He thought that Eunice Henderson's mother had a lot of money,' she was saying, staring into the depths of the cup. 'He was wrong, as it happens; the old woman was broke, she lost all her fortune in the Megatherium crash. Eunice has money of her own. She was supporting her mother. He read Eunice all wrong,' she added thoughtfully. 'She didn't like her mother—well, no one could—but she was content to wait until nature took its course. She didn't want to kill the old lady. I think that Alastair expected Eunice to be grateful, not mournful. He certainly didn't expect her to hire me to find out who killed her. That upset him. I thought he was just jealous of me because I seduced his friend.'

'Here, I say, Phryne!' objected Lindsay, waking up a little. Dot was smiling at him. Mr. Butler was refilling his glass. The policeman, who had evidently dressed in a hurry, as the bottoms of his pyjamas were visible beneath his trouser hems, was unmoved. Lindsay subsided. He was too tired, anyway, to worry about the rags of Miss Fisher's reputation.

'But I was wrong. He wasn't jealous—at least, not in that way. He was annoyed that any woman could take him on—could be so impudent as to attempt to fathom his motives! But I did. I caught sight of that guard's face, you know, and even with the scar and the cap I almost knew him. Then when he produced that alibi I was convinced that I must have been wrong, and then Lindsay exploded his Mills Bomb right under my chair. They are identical to a physical description.'

'You should have seen it,' said Lindsay sleepily. 'She swung down the boathouse porch like a monkey and drove back here like a demon. It was like riding the whirlwind.'

'Well, I didn't think we had time to spare.' Phryne drained the Irish coffee, touched her throat, and winced. 'And we didn't, either. Are the girls all right?'

'Yes, Miss, I checked, both as cosy as bugs in a rug, them and their cat.' Dot took one of Phryne's feet into her lap and began to rub it. She was sensible of the fact that while there were two sets of masculine arms to fall into, and one of them her current pet, Phryne had fallen into Dot's. Phryne's beautiful feet were colder than stone. Dot rubbed assiduously.

'I found out how he knew that little Jane knew him, Miss Fisher,' admitted Jack Robinson, vainly attempting to haul up his pyjama hem without seeming obvious. 'He overheard our conversation. My end of it, I mean, he was at the counter, signing the bail book, when I was talking to you. It won't happen again, I tell you,' he added fiercely. 'They will have to give me a phone in my office when I tell 'em about this. You could have been killed, Miss, not to mention the girls. What happened when you got to the house?'

'Well, I knew that he wasn't far ahead of us, because he'd been at the boathouse earlier, and I also knew that he could not get into the house. I had those windows fitted with strong diagonal bars, ever since Ember arrived and I realized how dark and little overlooked that sideway is. I thought that he would be prowling about the house, seeking whom he might devour.' She shuddered and swallowed painfully. 'And I thought that Lindsay and I would be a match for him. And we almost weren't, eh, Lindsay?'

'If you hadn't shot him,' opined Lindsay, 'he would have killed me. And I'm his oldest friend. Makes a man think, that does. Will he live, Detective-inspector?' Jack Robinson laughed grimly. Three o'clock in the morning was not his favourite hour, and he was not in the mood to mince words.

'He'll live to hang. Miss Fisher wasn't trying to kill him, so she didn't. He's got the constitution of an ox.'

At that moment, the telephone rang. Mr. Butler went to answer it. 'Miss Henderson, Miss Fisher,' he intoned. Phryne leaned on Dot's arm and staggered out to the phone.

'Hello, Eunice, what can I do for you?'

Phryne listened for a long moment; she thought that they might have been cut off. Then Eunice whispered, 'You know who killed Mother, don't you, Phryne?'

'Yes, my dear, I know.'

'I know too. It was Alastair, wasn't it?'

'Yes.'

'I knew his back, you see. I saw that blond guard, and I didn't recognize the face or the voice, but I knew his back. I've known all along, Phryne, and hoped it wasn't true.'

'Yes, Eunice.'

'Have they caught him?' The whisper was desperate.

'Yes, they've caught him.'

'Why?'

The voice was a wail. Phryne was too tired to think of a tactful reply, and talking hurt her throat.

'Money.'

'And Mother didn't have anything to leave but this house.' Eunice began to laugh. 'I would have given him everything I had.' There was a pause. 'Well, that's the end of that,' she said sadly.

'Eunice, have you no one to stay with you?' urged Phryne.

'No, dear, I don't need anyone. I shall be all right. I am on my own now—no mother, no relatives, no lover. It might be a rather interesting experience. I won't keep you in the hall on this cold night, Phryne. Thank you for everything.'

'Goodnight,' said Phryne, and Eunice hung up.

'That was Eunice Henderson,' she told her company. 'It seems that she suspected it was Alastair all along. Well, that's the end of that, as Eunice says. Give me some more of that Irish coffee, Mr. B., and then I think that we can all go to bed, again.'

'You'll be in touch, Miss Fisher? Have to make a statement about the capture of the felon,' said Jack Robinson. 'Nice work, Miss Fisher. We shall have to get you in the force, ha, ha.'

'Ha, ha,' agreed Phryne waspishly. 'Is it proved by evidence, Jack? Have some of the coffee, it puts heart into you. Are you all right, Lindsay?'

'Yes, I'm all right, just a little dazed by the pace of events.'

Phryne laughed. Jack Robinson accepted a cup of Irish coffee and said, 'Yes, well, they found the old woman's rings in his rooms. He escaped without leaving any traces, you know. He leapt down from the water tower onto the old woman's body, and thence to the track; there weren't no mud on him, so he didn't leave a mark. Then he coiled up his rope, walked down the track to the next station, changed his clothes and dumped the guard's uniform and the cap, peeled off his scar, and put on his own clothes again—he was carrying them all the time, in a knapsack like soldiers use. Relic of his climbing days, I assume. Then he took the train back to town. It was a good plot, though stagey. We might never have laid a hand on him if it weren't for you, Miss Fisher. I hope that you are not too uncomfortable.'

'Uncomfortable? No, not really, though I am going to be as stiff as a board tomorrow. Lindsay, my dear, you must have suspected him. You lived in the same house. He must have spouted all that guff about the superman to you.'

Lindsay woke up a little, blinking.

'Oh, yes, he did, Phryne, but I never paid much attention to it, I mean, one's friends often make asses of themselves, and it does not do to hold it against them. I thought that it was a phase he was going through—medical men are often odd, you know.'

'Yes, I know.'

'And what will happen to those two girls?' asked Jack Robinson. 'Shall I call in the Welfare?'

'No!' protested Phryne. 'They will be fine with me. I shall send them both to school, and they shall go to university if they wish. They're good girls,' she added quietly. 'Besides, Bert will kill me if anything happens to them. They will be fine. No need to worry about them.'

'Then I won't worry, and I will leave you,' said the detective-inspector. 'It's late and the missus will be worrying. Good night, Miss Fisher. Sleep well,' he added, with a wicked sidelong glance at Lindsay. Mr. Butler saw him out and doused the outside light. Phryne Fisher was not at home to any more visitors tonight.

Dot assisted Phryne to her feet. She held out a bruised hand to the beautiful Lindsay.

'Will you come and sleep with me?' she asked softly.

Lindsay attempted to leap to his feet, emitted a sharp gasp, and allowed Dot to drag him out of the chair.

Dot conducted the two of them upstairs into Phryne's boudoir, and put them to bed together neatly. She fetched an extra pillow for the young man and narrowly restrained herself from kissing his cheek as she tucked him in. Phryne was already asleep as soon as she lay down, and had embraced the young man, laying her head on his shoulder. He looked up at Dot, smiling drowsily.

'Good night, Dot,' he slurred, blind with fatigue, and this time Dot stooped and kissed him.

'Sweet dreams,' said Dot, extinguishing the light and closing the door.

She climbed her own stairs and found her own bed, but was not sleepy. She thought of the murder, the horrible transformation of the young man into a monster, and the tragic history of the two girls bedded down with their kitten in the guest bedroom. All the while, as she looked out to sea from her uncurtained window, the lights that were ships moved unfalteringly across the invisible water as if drawn by threads. Dot sighed, took off her dressing-gown and climbed into her own narrow bed.

There must be a reason in it all, thought Dot, and fell asleep trying to think of one.

To receive a free catalog of Poisoned Pen Press titles, please contact us in one of the following ways:

Phone: 1-800-421-3976
Facsimile: 1-480-949-1707
E-mail: info@poisonedpenpress.com
Website: www.poisonedpenpress.com

Poisoned Pen Press
6962 E. First Ave. Ste. 103
Scottsdale, AZ 85251